Chesapeake
Bay
Christmas

Narielle Living
Jackie Guidry
Jeanne Johansen

Christmas Tales from the Bay Sisters

CHESAPEAKE BAY CHRISTMAS

ISBN: 978-0-6157286-3-6

Published by High Tide Publications (HighTidePublications.com)

First Edition November, 2012

Printed in the United States of America

Dedication

This book is dedicated to our families.

Thank you for believing in us.

About the authors:

Jackie Guidry

Jackie Guidry is a paranormal historical fiction author who loves folktales and legends. As current Vice-President of the Chesapeake Bay Writers, Jackie assists in judging the All-Stars writing contest, coordinates events and workshops, and contributes to the club's newsletter. A military wife and mother of two wonderful children, Jackie is finishing her first novel about Mahlah and the crossroads. She lives and writes near Virginia's Chesapeake Bay. Visit **www.jackieguidry.com** for book release updates, contests and writing tips.

Narielle Living

Narielle Living is a regularly featured writer for the Hampton Roads magazine **Next Door Neighbor**, and has published hundreds of articles for online sites such as ehow.com, DIY.com and HyperInk. In 2011 and 2009 she won third and second place respectively for her short stories in the Yorktown Library Literary Competition. She is a board member of the Chesapeake Bay Writers and a member of Sisters In Crime. Her mysteries, **Signs of the South** and **Past Unfinished** are available from Pulse Publishing on Amazon and Barnes & Noble. More information can be found **at www.narielleliving.com**.

Jeanne Johansen

Jeanne Johansen is a historical mystery writer. A technical writer in the medical field with many Internet articles to her credit,

Jeanne began as editor and publisher of a neighborhood newspaper when she was six years old. She belongs to the Chesapeake Bay Writers Groups, Virginia Writers Club, and Sisters in Crime. She lives in Deltaville, Virginia, with her husband, Carl. Her mystery **27 Minutes** is available from Pulse Publishing on Amazon and Barnes & Noble. She has a new novel **The Diary of Priscilla Llewlyn Doyle** is scheduled for release in March 2013. More information can be found at **www.JM-Johansen.com**.

A Family for Christmas

By

Narielle Living

She caught the dark shape out of the corner of her eye, while the scrutiny of someone burned on her back. Every now and then she heard a soft exhale. Zoe knew without question that she was being followed.

The busy department store boasted an array of glittering Christmas decorations with piped-in music reminding shoppers to be merry. Halloween was barely a memory, but the holiday smell of cinnamon and evergreens wafted through the space. With temperatures still hovering in the 70s, it was holiday time in Virginia.

Through the haze of forced holiday cheer, Zoe saw her two foot tall stalker playing peek-a-boo from inside the skirt rack in the juniors department.

"Are you following me?" Zoe demanded.

A bright, dimpled smile answered her. It looked like her young shadow wasn't even old enough to talk.

Zoe looked around, trying to find the child's parents. Nobody was paying attention to the little girl, but maybe her family was busy shopping.

"Where's your mommy, honey?"

Somber eyes looked up at Zoe and the small head shook from side to side.

"No? Does that mean you don't know where they are? Are you lost?" Zoe's heart melted at the sight of this adorable little girl standing in the misses' clothes rack. Large hazel eyes stared up from a round face framed by blonde curls.

"Why don't you come on out of there, your parents might be looking for you." Zoe held her hand out to the child, who immediately ran to her and threw her arms around Zoe's legs. Without hesitation, Zoe lifted the child into her arms.

"Okay, kiddo, I know you didn't drive here by yourself. Let's see if we can't find who you belong to."

Zoe walked through the store with the child in her arms, hoping someone would spot them and come running over. "Let me know when you see someone from your family. I'm sure they're frantic by now." As they wandered, the little girl let loose with a stream of babble. It was impossible to know what the child was telling her, but the animated gestures and conversational patter made Zoe smile.

"My goodness, I'll bet you are just the smartest little girl ever, aren't you?" A moment of silence echoed the child's agreement. "Look, we're in the men's department already. Maybe your Daddy's here and he just lost track of you."

***

David stood in the men's department, looking at ties while his mind was busy with family affairs. Driving to the mall after visiting his sister Rhonda and her husband Pete, he'd experienced a mixture of love and disdain for them. He loved his sister, he really did, but he couldn't understand their lifestyle. Pete was a low paid carpenter, while Rhonda was a stay at home mother to multitudes of children that were not her own.

Pete and Rhonda's habit of caring for foster children was reflected in their home furnishings. Shabby and well-worn, the furniture withstood years of children jumping, drooling and God knew what else.

I wish they would at least let me buy them a new living room set. It's so embarrassing to see how they live, in that tiny little house, but Rhonda won't listen to me. Ever. She just laughs every time I suggest it.

Absently fingering the multi-colored ties on the rack in front of him, David looked up to notice a perky young woman with a child in her arms. Staring at Zoe, he froze.

I know her.

He must have seen her somewhere before, but he couldn't think where. A rush of heat raced through him as he stared at the shoulder length red hair curling around her face.

Why does she look so familiar? Am I having a moment of déjà-vu?

She was what would be described as interesting looking, dressed in a bright, bohemian style that was the exact opposite of what David looked for in a woman. The hippy-dippy style was not for him.

She's beautiful.

He was confused by his reaction; David was not the type of man to indulge in an instant attraction, regardless of the woman, but especially attraction toward someone with a style like that. He preferred sleek, not folksy.

Perhaps he'd seen her at this mall before, or shopping somewhere else. That would explain why he thought he knew her. No reason to get all worked up over some strange woman.

Still, she intrigued him.

Her voice skipped across the store. "Look at all the Christmas decorations. Let's see, these ornaments over here are red, and this is blue... just give a holler when you see Daddy or someone, okay honey?"

Envy settled into David as he listened to the woman's chatter, and watched the perfect picture of mother and daughter.

***

Searching the aisles of each department, Zoe's apprehension mounted. The parents were nowhere to be found. "This is weird. Who leaves a kid alone in the middle of the mall?" As the girl's grip tightened around her neck, Zoe bit her lip. She hadn't meant to say that out loud.

Good thing I found her. There are lots of weird people in this world, and it's dangerous for a little girl to be alone in a mall.

A line of customers waited at the nearest cash register. Saturday was the busiest shopping day of the week, and today was no exception. Trying to catch the attention of the teenaged cashier, she stepped to the front of the line.

Shoppers responded immediately.

"Hey, no cutting!"

"Get to the end of the line, lady."

Zoe looked at the people in line, telling them, "I'm not buying anything, I just have a question."

"Yeah, well park your question in back," shot a disgruntled man waiting his turn.

Zoe's arms circled the child tighter, holding her in a protective embrace. "This is important, so I'm sure you can spare the thirty seconds it will take." Turning to the pierced cashier she asked, "I have a lost child here. Has anybody come by who's lost a child, or reported anything about a missing child?"

"You'll have to go to the mall security. That's on the other side of the building, down where they've got Santa set up."

"Santa's here?" Zoe was surprised. Thanksgiving was still weeks away.

"I think your thirty seconds are up," snarled the customer in line.

"There's no need to be rude." The voice was behind her.

Surprised, Zoe looked up at the man who came to her defense. Dressed in an expensive suit, he looked every bit the handsome and imposing executive type. She'd worked with men like this and tended to avoid dealing with these high powered people. Nothing good ever happened when she did business with them.

"Oh, and I suppose you want to cut into the line, too," said the customer.

Nothing like a little bit of Christmas to bring out the best in people.

"No," her new friend responded evenly. "I just don't think you have any reason to be rude to a woman and her child."

Her stomach did a flip when he looked down at her and asked, "Are you alright? Is there anything I can help you with?"

Staring into his deep blue eyes set in a classically chiseled face, Zoe had trouble finding words.

He's here.

Her immediate reaction was confusing, to say the least.

"Thank you, I'm, I mean, we're fine. We're leaving," she stammered. Heart pounding against her rib cage, she suppressed a shiver when he placed his hand on the small of her back, leading her away from the crowd and toward the door.

"It seems that people are getting a head start on their holiday rudeness," he said, frowning. Reaching the store exit that led into the mall interior, they stopped.

"Well, umm, thanks. I appreciate your concern." At that moment the child in her arms began to babble again, kicking her legs and reaching her arms out toward him.

He smiled at the little girl. "Hello, princess. Are you having a good time shopping with your mommy?"

"Oh," Zoe breathed. "I'm not her mom. I found her back in the girls department, and I think she must be lost because there's nobody around looking for her. I was trying to find out where to go to help find her parents." There was a brief moment of silence as they looked at the bright little girl, happily babbling in her own language.

"I mean, somebody must be looking for her, right?" Zoe needed confirmation of this, and surely the man standing in front of her would know something. Suits like him always did.

"I would think so," he answered. "But I admit, that is a little disconcerting. Do you want me to go with you? I can help you straighten all this out."

Zoe hesitated. Although she felt a strong attraction to this very handsome stranger, she also knew that that was exactly what he was – a stranger. The child in her arms changed everything, and she couldn't wander off with the first good looking man to come along. Even one in a suit. For all she knew, he could be something terrible, like a serial killer or a stock broker.

As if sensing her hesitation, he added, "Listen, my name is David Russell. I'm a vice president over at Eastboard Communications. Why don't I just walk with you to the security office?"

Zoe decided to go with what her instincts were telling her and to trust him. Besides, she was surrounded by people and wouldn't be going alone with him. They would stay in the mall where it was safe.

"Thanks, that'd be nice. I'm Zoe Dearborn, president of Zoe's Extraordinary Beads." She said the last part with a faint smile, knowing that he wasn't the kind of man that would be familiar with her product.

They walked in silence through the mall, David keeping his hand firmly on the small of Zoe's back, Zoe with the child held protectively in her arms. For some reason, this didn't bother Zoe. In fact, she liked it, the warm feeling of his hand on her. Even dressed the way he was, Mr. David Russell was a handsome man.

What am I thinking? I don't pick up men at the mall. I don't pick up men, period.

Her day had taken a decidedly unusual turn.

For a brief moment, she wondered if people thought they were a family. Trying to stop that line of thinking and break her discomfort, Zoe asked, "So, what does Eastboard Communications do?"

"Global marketing strategies. What does Zoe's Extraordinary Beads do?" He asked the question without disdain, but it still made Zoe defensive.

"I make beaded jewelry, necklaces, earrings, that kind of thing."

David nodded, his face serious under the fluorescent lights. "And what does your husband do?" he asked.

Zoe bristled at the question. "What makes you think I'm married?"

"Well, you must be if that beading business is your only job. I can't imagine you could support yourself doing that. Can you?"

"For your information, yes I can, and I do very well thank you."

"I didn't mean to insult you, I just –"

"I know," Zoe interrupted, stopping in the middle of the mall. "High powered executives like you could not imagine living life the way I do. I'll bet you have a nice foreign car, and a nice condo, with the kind of furniture that's all sleek and modern. You probably take a vacation twice a year and have a girlfriend or wife that's tall and knows how to throw a proper dinner party. I'm sure you couldn't imagine living in a small apartment but absolutely loving your career, or not buying designer labels but buying from a thrift shop because they have more interesting clothes."

David looked like he was trying not to smile. "Do you have a cat, too?" he asked.

Zoe fumed.

"I will not even bother to answer that question. You should probably leave now." Turning on her heel, Zoe marched toward the door to the security office. It didn't matter that she did, in fact, have a cat. What mattered was the impudence with which he had asked her.

The security guard standing outside the office greeted Zoe, while David stood a few yards back. *Good. Who needs him?* Without warning, the little girl in her arms let loose with a piercing wail that could be heard the entire length of the mall. Her chubby little arms reached back to David.

Zoe froze. She wasn't experienced enough with children to know what this meant, and it looked like the kid was in pain. "What's wrong, honey?" she asked the little girl. She tried jiggling the child and patting her on the back, but the screams continued.

"Babababa. Ba."

"Oh, well that makes sense, then."

"Is there a problem here?" the security guard asked

"No, I mean, yes." Zoe was flustered. The child's reaction to David, combined with the frustration Zoe felt toward the man and the ache in her arms made her lightheaded.

"What she means is that she would like to report a lost child." David stepped forward and the child looked at him with obvious delight in her eyes.

"Just because he's handsome doesn't mean you need to fawn over him," Zoe whispered to the child. The little girl batted her eyes at David, causing Zoe to sigh.

"Did you lose your child?" the guard asked.

"No, I found this child in a department store. I looked for her parents, but I couldn't find them, so I came here."

"Whose child is that?"

Zoe looked at David, realizing that the security guard was a little slow to understand the situation.

"We don't know, we were hoping you could help us find out," David answered carefully. Turning to Zoe, he told her, "Listen, I'm sorry, I didn't mean to insult you back there. Please accept my apologies."

"I suppose." Zoe wasn't sure if she was more upset with him or with herself for feeling so attracted to him. It wasn't right that she felt an overwhelming urge to throw herself at him, but that wasn't his fault. Besides, if the kid was any indication, Zoe wasn't the only female wanting to throw herself at him.

The guard shrugged and turned. "Yeah, sure, I'll make an announcement." Moments later his voice was heard over the mall's loudspeaker. "Attention, everyone. A lost child has been found. Will the parents of the child please report to the security office. A lost child has been found. Parents, please report to the security office."

David and Zoe stood, awkwardly, waiting for someone to claim the child. Zoe's arms tightened briefly as she thought about the parents that might claim her. *Where on earth are they, and why aren't they frantically searching for her already? If this were my child, I would be out of my mind with worry by now.*

As if on cue, David frowned at Zoe and said, "I can't believe her parents aren't already here, or haven't at least checked with security."

The guard answered. "Well, no one has stopped by to report a missing child. If no one steps forward to claim this one, I'm going to have to call the police."

***

The police officer taking the report shuffled his feet and didn't make much eye contact. He was clearly uncomfortable.

"I know you care about what happens to the kid, but I need to get all the information before we can launch an investigation," he said.

"In the meantime, I'll take her for a walk around the mall, see if anyone is looking for her," David said. This little girl did not need to hear a police officer grilling Zoe. Besides, what if her parents were in another store, still searching? Unlikely, but possible. Maybe they hadn't heard the earlier announcement.

"I'm sorry, I need you to stay here for now. Rules are rules," the officer said for the fourth time.

"Some rules inhibit progress," Zoe said, still clutching the girl.

"I'm sure her parents wouldn't want a stranger walking around with their kid," the officer said. "Now, what did you do between the time you left the store where you found her and the time you got here?"

David marveled at Zoe's composure, listening as she answered the same question for the third time. Personally, he wanted to rip the note pad out of the officer's hand, but that would be counterproductive.

Still, it would feel good to at least be doing something.

"Alright folks, I think I have enough information," the officer said. "Now we just have to wait for the social worker to get here and then we can all be on our way."

Zoe's face was a mask, but David suspected she was trying not to cry. After all, this was not their child and they knew that. Somewhere, someone had to be missing the little girl.

David cleared his throat. "Perhaps while we wait we can take the child to get some lunch. It is, after all, getting late in the day, and I'm sure she's hungry."

As if in response, the child kicked her legs and squealed, making Zoe laugh. "David, I think that's a great idea. Let's go get her some food, and the social worker can meet us at the restaurant." She turned to the officer and pointed to where they would be eating. "Right there, you can see the restaurant from here. Just tell the social worker where he can find us." Without waiting for a response, she turned and began to walk away.

"Ma'am?" the police officer called after her. "Ma'am, I'm not sure this is such a good idea. Why don't we all wait here for the social worker?"

Zoe stared at him with a steely glint in her eyes. "Officer, I understand that you have a job to do, but this child needs food. The restaurant is only a few steps away from us. Surely you are not going to let her be neglected, are you?"

David suppressed a smile as he watched the officer stammer. "Of course not, you go right ahead. I'll make sure he knows where you are."

Following Zoe, David couldn't help but realize that his admiration for the woman had grown substantially. Not only was he attracted to her physically, but he loved her natural maternal instinct. She didn't hand the kid over to someone else to take care of, a trait he knew he might find in other women he associated with.

Once seated in the restaurant, he asked, "Do you have children of your own? You seem like such a natural mom."

Blushing, Zoe looked down at the table. "No. I've always wanted a family, but it just never happened."

"Don't you have a boyfriend?"

"Not right now. Besides, at this point it's probably too late."

David was puzzled. "Too late for a boyfriend?"

"No, too late for a family. I'm going to be thirty nine years old in December."

"That's not too old. I'm the same age, and I'm still planning on having a family."

"Oh. Do you have a girlfriend, then?"

David hesitated. He knew he needed to tell her the truth, but he didn't want to. His better instincts won. "Yes. Stephanie and I have been dating for quite some time now. Her father works at my company."

"Hmm. I'll bet she'll make a good corporate wife then, right?"

David was unreasonably annoyed. His relationship with Stephanie was none of her business. "Stephanie has a career of her own. She's not the type to sit at home and become a corporate executive's wife." David hoped his tone was enough to stop the questions, but apparently not.

"I see. And what does, um, Sofie do for a living?"

"Stephanie. She's a media relations consultant."

"Right. Stephanie." The food arrived, and Zoe was busy cutting the child's chicken into small pieces. "Here sweetheart, do you know how to use a spoon? I'll help you with the applesauce."

David was silent, watching Zoe feed the little girl. "What do you think her name is?"

"Abigail."

"Wow, that was quick. What made you think of that?"

Zoe shrugged. "I don't know, it just seems like I've been thinking of her as Abby. You know, short for Abigail. She looks like that would be her name."

David stared at the child. Zoe was right; she did look like an Abby. "Okay, then let's call her Abby."

Zoe's face was wistful. "At least we can call her that for as long as she's with us. What do you think will happen?"

David hesitated. A piece of an idea had come to him while they were talking to the police, but he didn't want to say anything. Instead, he was waiting for the social worker.

"I don't want to say too much to get your hopes up, but I may have an idea."

"Do you think they'll let her come home with me?" David knew that Zoe was trying hard not to cry, especially in front of Abby. She wouldn't let the little girl see her dismay.

David hated to tell her, but he had to be honest. He hoped Zoe would think this was an attractive quality, but it was probably too soon for him to think about that. He had no right, yet, to pursue a relationship. "No, I doubt it. That's not usually how social services operates."

"Indeed it's not. Indeed." David and Zoe looked up from their meal to find an older, round and slightly disheveled man standing before them.

David blinked. He'd never seen a man quite so... gray. Clothes and hair David could understand, but this guy's skin had a washed out tone, as if he never went outside, or lived under fluorescent lights only.

"Forgive the interruption, but I assume you two are um, let me see…" Pulling a pair of half spectacles down from a graying head of hair, he removed a piece of paper from his bulging briefcase and read, "Zoe Dearborn and David Russell?" At their affirmative nods, he smiled and extended a hand to Zoe and David in turn.

David shook his hand, feeling comfortable with the social worker despite his unfortunate coloring.

"Wonderful, lovely to meet you both, truly wonderful," he boomed. "I'm Percy, the case worker assigned to you. Why don't we just sit and talk for a moment."

Percy sat next to David in the booth, smiling at Abby. "Well, hello there. What are we eating today?"

Abby's face broke into a large smile and she began chattering away to the man, waving her forkful of chicken as she spoke. Percy listened for a moment, nodding. "I see," he told her. Turning to Zoe and David, he said, "Our young friend here says you have been taking very good care of her. Let's talk about what's going to happen next."

David cleared his throat before speaking. "Actually, Percy, I kind of have an idea."

***

The sun had set long before David arrived home. His condominium was situated on the water, providing spectacular views of Virginia Beach. Pulling into his garage, it hit him. He didn't look out his windows anymore, he didn't see the sunrises over the water that the realtor had promised he'd love or the sweep of white sand just beyond his doorstep. His mornings were focused on getting to work on time, so he no longer heard the cry of the gulls outside or smelled the salt in the air. And the rest of his days were just as busy, too.

It's late and it's dark and I paid a huge amount of money for a place I barely live in. It's all for show. Zoe was right about me.

Exhausted, he climbed the steps into his living space, took off his coat and threw it over a dining room chair. Loosening his tie, he sank into the couch, throwing his head back onto the cushions and shutting his eyes.

"Don't close your eyes just yet, darling. We have reservations tonight, remember? Where on earth have you been, anyway?"

Keeping his eyes closed, David answered. "Stephanie, can't we just eat in tonight? Maybe have a home cooked meal for a change?"

He felt her pout before he saw it. Standing at the granite topped island that separated the kitchen from the living space, his girlfriend impatiently tapped her manicured nails.

"David, what are you talking about? We're supposed to go to the opening of the new Cambodian restaurant downtown tonight. It's important for us to go, we need to be seen. Why on earth would you want some sort of dreary home cooked meal, anyway? What's gotten into you?"

Sighing, he opened his eyes and got up from the couch. Walking to her, he planted a kiss on her cheek. "You're right. I'm just tired. It's been a long and really weird day."

Stephanie's cat-like green eyes narrowed at him. Standing at five feet nine inches in her stiletto heels, she wore an obviously expensive little black dress for the evening. "You must have visited your sister."

Irritation flashed through David. "Yes, that was part of it. She's doing well, by the way, and sends her regards."

"I'm sure. How are all the little monsters?"

Normally David would find this amusing, but tonight was different. For the first time in a long time, he was offended on behalf of his sister. "They're okay, you know, they're just kids. Rhonda and Pete do the best they can with them."

Stephanie shuddered. "I cannot imagine having all those children climbing all over my house. Anyway, do hurry dear, we don't want to be late."

David stopped, staring at his girlfriend. She hadn't changed; she was still the same woman she had always been. Beautiful, sophisticated and a bit of a snob, Stephanie was what he always thought he wanted in a woman. *Maybe I've changed. Maybe this whole crazy day has somehow changed who I am. For better or worse, now's the time to get this out in the open.*

"Stephanie, I know we've never talked about this before, but I need to ask you something."

"Now?"

"Yes, now."

"Is this going to be a marriage proposal?" Stephanie's eyes glittered.

"No, but it's something we need to discuss if we're thinking about marriage. Would you ever be interested in starting a family, having children?"

Stephanie took a long, slow breath before answering. "David, you know that my career is the most important part of my life right now." Seeing the look on his face, she hurried to add, "Outside of you, of course."

"Of course," he muttered.

"I have to say that I don't see myself staying home, playing mommy, stewing tomatoes every day and wiping up snot and God knows what else. I thought you understood that, my career comes first. And now that it looks like I'll be up for another promotion, well, even if I wanted children, I just don't think I'd have the time."

"I see." And he did. David understood exactly what Stephanie was saying, that she had not in fact changed at all. He also realized something important about himself.

"Well, Steph, I want a family. I want kids, and I would love to have a wife who stayed home to care for them. I won't settle for less."

Stephanie stared at him coolly. "Then, David, I would say that you and I have a problem. A serious problem."

***

"So it's over, just like that?" Rhonda's excited voice bounced through the phone lines.

"Thanks for the show of sympathy, sis," David said. "Anyway, I'm sorry to be calling so late, I hope I didn't wake you." It was after eleven, but he'd taken a chance his sister was still awake. "I had to let you know everything that happened today so you'd be ready for tomorrow."

"Oh, don't worry, everything is all set. Abby is here right now. She's asleep."

"Already?" David was surprised. He'd hoped his sister could take Abby, but he knew that sometimes regulations and legal restrictions prevailed.

"Yeah, I guess Percy was pretty impressed when he checked our records because he called us right away. I almost couldn't believe the story he told me. Is it true you were at the mall with a woman and you two just found this little thing? All by herself?"

"Well, that's sort of how it happened. Actually, Zoe found Abby, I just found Zoe."

"Zoe?"

"Yes, and she's a really great person. In fact, I think you're going to like her when you meet her."

David knew his sister would embrace Zoe in a way she'd never been able to do with Stephanie. For one thing, Zoe was much warmer, nicer, prettier…

"I get to meet her? Is this the real reason why you broke up with Stephanie?" Rhonda's voice intruded.

The image of Zoe was already in David's head, her red hair and creamy skin, her soft curves and delicious scent. After only the short amount of time he'd spent with her, he couldn't stop thinking about the woman. He'd never known this kind of attraction, and wasn't sure what to do with it.

"David?" his sister interrupted his thoughts.

"No, Stephanie and I had a little talk, and I guess I figured out that we're not as compatible as I thought we were."

"Well, hallelujah to that is what I say." Rhonda's voice was firm. "She was no good for you. So, if this Zoe has nothing to do with your break up, why am I going to meet her?"

"She got really attached to Abby today, and I think she feels responsible for what happens to the little girl. And I wanted to warn you, she's applying to become a foster parent, too. She wants Abby to live with her."

"Did she tell you that she wanted Abby to live with her?" Rhonda asked.

"She didn't exactly put it into words, but I saw the look on her face when Percy took Abby away. I think it kind of tore her up inside. She just turned to me and started crying."

"Poor kid," Rhonda's voice was sympathetic. "I know how it is, you get attached to the little ones and then something happens. I hope it works out, for her sake."

David was startled to realize what a generous woman Rhonda was. Most people would be selfishly worried about their own claim on the child, but with a rare flash of insight he realized his sister wasn't like that. She'd want only what was best for Abby.

How could anyone not want that child to have the best of everything? She was sweet and innocent, and sure as hell didn't deserve being abandoned in a shopping mall.

His sister's voice broke into his thoughts. "Of course Zoe can come over anytime, I'd love to meet her. Does she know where we live?"

David hesitated. "Actually, she asked me to pick her up tomorrow and take her to your house. I hope that's okay with you."

Rhonda laughed. "Good, she's a mama bear who knows what she wants. Well, you can come on over any time after breakfast. We'll be here."

David was touched, and maybe even a little embarrassed. "Thanks, Rhonda. I'll see you tomorrow." Perhaps he'd been wrong about his sister all these years.

***

Zoe's neighborhood in Norfolk was sometimes referred to as transitional. Not quite the outskirts of town where crime and poverty reigned, but close enough to the edges of that to maintain that simultaneous juxtaposition of shabby yet vibrant. Lawns weren't always mowed, but neighborhood grocers offered a wider variety of ethnic foods not carried by the local chains. House colors ranged from white to shocking blue, as there was no historical zoning in effect here to keep everything muted. Zoe's house was divided into three apartments, and the rent from the two tenants mostly paid her mortgage. Decorated in a style that was pure Zoe, it was her sanctuary.

Curled on her couch, Zoe stared at the night sky outside her window. She knew she had work to do, but couldn't get motivated. Despite what David had hinted at earlier, Zoe's Extraordinary Beads did a tremendous business. Her three full time employees and two part time employees kept pace with the steady flow of orders. The success of the business was due largely to her outrageous designs; Zoe Dearborn was known for successfully pairing unlikely colors and using non-traditional design patterns in her work. Her artistic talent was evident in her creations, her common sense helped build a successful business.

Tonight, though, her mind was preoccupied with thoughts of two people: Abby and David. It was obvious to her why she was consumed with thoughts of the little girl, after all, she was a child all alone in the world. How did that happen? How did she end up alone in a mall, with no one to claim her? Was there an irresponsible baby-sitter or nanny involved? Zoe shuddered at the thought of anyone else finding the girl. *There's lots of weird people out there, thank God I found her when I did.*

Her other thoughts were more confusing. The feelings David evoked were unexpected, to say the least. She had a great time with him, and loved the way he made her feel. Despite the obvious physical attraction, she loved that David expressed an interest in her thoughts and opinions during lunch. They had talked late into the afternoon, even after Percy had taken Abby to her foster home.

"I can't believe he has a sister that takes care of foster children," Zoe told her tortoise-shell colored cat who lay curled against her. "Maybe I shouldn't have been so dismissive of him and his whole corporate lifestyle."

She closed her eyes and rubbed them. Whatever attraction she felt for the man didn't matter anyway. He had a girlfriend, so that was the end of that. Zoe was not a woman who went after other people's men, and she wasn't interested in being with someone who cheated.

Absently petting her cat, the burn of unshed tears stung her eyes. "It's so weird, I almost felt like we were a real family. I miss Abby, but I miss David, too. How could I have feelings for him so quickly?"

At least the cat listens to me. Reaching for a bag of chips, Zoe said, "I have a feeling this is going to be a very long night."

*****

Zoe was unable to sleep, and finally gave up and got out of bed as the first light of dawn crept into her room. Taking her time, she had a leisurely breakfast and read the morning newspaper from cover to cover, including the classifieds. Her cat watched silently from his window perch, ears periodically twitching at something Zoe would read aloud.

"There's nothing in here, nothing at all. I don't know why I thought there would be," she announced to the feline as she refolded the paper. "I guess I had an image of a front page article, something that said, 'Little Girl Missing, Mother Frantic'. They must not have found her family yet."

Again, Zoe wondered about that. There had to be someone out there who cared about the girl. If Zoe had ever wandered off in a store when she was a kid her mother would've torn the place apart looking for her.

Telling herself there was no real reason for it, Zoe took extra care as she got ready for the day. She picked a flattering outfit to wear, a long, slim green skirt topped with a soft, cream sweater that hugged her curves. She was careful to use the right products on her hair and applied just the right amount of makeup.

"Not that it matters," she reminded herself. "He's got a girlfriend."

At exactly eleven that morning, her doorbell rang. Looking out the peephole, she saw a smiling David waving at her. Opening the door, she laughed. "How did you know I was looking through the peep hole?"

"It's what I expected you to do," he answered, entering her apartment. He seemed at ease, his presence filling the space. It was hard for her to breathe with him taking up all the air around her. "Are you ready to go?"

Zoe nervously took in David's casual look, jeans and a sweater with a brown leather jacket. He smelled good, too, a combination of some type of soap and cologne.

"I'm ready when you are," she said, and immediately blushed, realizing that her statement could be misinterpreted.

"I'm ready right now," David whispered, taking a step toward her. Without warning, he leaned over and allowed his lips to meet hers. His kiss was gentle at first, softly grazing her lips. There was no mistaking the intent.

Zoe took a step back, reeling. "Okay, wow. What was that all about? Don't you have a girlfriend, Sandy or something?"

David's face was serious as he looked into her eyes. "No. Her name was Stephanie, but we split up."

"Really? And exactly when did that happen?" Zoe wasn't born yesterday, and she wasn't about to let herself get duped into a relationship with a cheater.

"It happened last night when I got home. We had a little conversation about what we wanted out of life and decided it was time to go our separate ways. I think it was a long time coming, I just hadn't realized it. Now, are you ready to go see Abby?"

Zoe stared at him for a moment, then consciously closed her mouth. She believed him about his break up, but wasn't certain what that meant for her. "Let's go," she said decisively. There would be plenty of time later to think about David and the fact that he was now single.

The drive to Rhonda's house didn't take long. David knocked, opened the door and entered. Rhonda was warm and welcoming, and they were barely inside the house when Abby ran to sit with Zoe, babbling non-stop in her own language.

"How did she sleep last night? Did she eat a good breakfast?" Zoe's anxiety about the girl's well-being was soon dispelled by Rhonda.

"She slept very well, and she ate a pretty big breakfast. She has a room all to herself, would you like to see it?"

Walking through the small house, Zoe couldn't help but admire this couple and all that they did. It was obvious that they didn't have a lot of money, but it seemed to Zoe that the feeling of warmth and comfort in their home more than made up for that fact.

"I love your sister and her husband, it's great here," she whispered to David a few minutes later.

With a wry smile, he answered, "I'm so glad you think so. It's taken me a while, but I have to agree with you."

"So what are you kids going to do today?" Rhonda called from the other room.

"Do?" David wasn't sure what she meant.

"Well, yes, silly. You three don't want to sit around here all day. Why don't you go to the park or something?" Rhonda walked back into the room with a bowl of chips. "There's no reason to hang out with us, you'll have more fun if you take Abby out for a while. What do you think, Pete?"

Her husband, Pete, answered with a smile toward his wife. "I think whatever you think, sweetheart."

"Take your coats, it's chilly outside. Just be sure to come back by four, that's when Percy's stopping by for a visit."

Bemused, Zoe and David got Abby into her coat and walked outside toward the car. Barely a moment passed before Rhonda opened the front door and called after them, "Don't forget to take the car seat out of my car for her."

***

Closing the door with a satisfied smile, Rhonda looked at her husband sitting in his chair across the room. "I don't know how it happened, but I feel like I just got my brother back. I think this is going to be perfect, don't you?"

Pete shook his head at her. "Don't get your little matchmaking hopes up yet. You never know. He could still change his mind and go back to life with Suzy."

"Stephanie."

"Whatever her name was. Your brother's a great guy, don't get me wrong, but he lives differently than us."

Rhonda wasn't listening. "It's obvious that they have feelings for each other, you can just tell when they're in the same room together. I mean, geez Louise, the air around them sizzles. Reminds me of one of them romance books. Maybe we can have a June wedding."

Pete didn't answer. He knew enough to know that he wasn't going to change his wife's mind. Besides, a June wedding was just fine with him.

***

Zoe couldn't remember the last time she had so much fun. The three of them walked through the park, stopping to play at the playground. David and Zoe climbed the equipment with Abby, and all three of them went down the slide. Later, they found a small snack shack that sold big, warm pretzels and laughed as they ordered first one, then another, and finally a third.

Walking around, Abby toddled in front of them, babbling and pointing at birds, people and trees. David reached for Zoe, holding her hand firmly.

"I like this," he told her.

"Me too." Zoe felt no apprehension about this man, but was pierced by a wave of longing so intense it took her breath away. Was it this man in particular she wanted, or was it the safety of a family? Part of her felt the need for caution, the need to protect herself from possible hurt. The other part of her wanted to run away with David.

"Maybe after we bring Abby home and talk to Percy we could get some dinner." David's voice sounded husky.

Zoe didn't hesitate. "That would be great. Your place or mine?" Her boldness surprised her, but then everything about this situation surprised her. She'd never known a man like David who had such a strong effect on her. She was comfortable with him, he made her laugh and she wanted him in a physical way that left her aching. Yep, she had it bad alright.

Leaning in to kiss her, David said, "I think that the way I feel right now even the car would be just fine."

"We'll go to your place, this way I'll get to see all that fancy chrome and granite."

"How do you know that's what my place looks like?"

Zoe smiled. "I already know lots about you, David."

"Good. Just as long as you understand that I'm planning on us getting to know each other even better. Much better."

***

David, Zoe and Abby got back to the house a little before four o'clock. Sitting in the living room, they laughed together as they told Rhonda about their day. At times, Rhonda had to ask what they were talking about, claiming she couldn't understand them because they were both talking at the same time, or one was laughing while the other spoke. Mixed in with this was Abby's excited chatter as she shared her own perspective on the afternoon.

A knock on the door stopped all conversation. Zoe's stomach tightened as Rhonda let Percy in. *Has he found them? Has he found Abby's parents?* Zoe's mind whirled with the ramifications of what that would mean for her. *If he did, I might never see Abby again.* Zoe knew the child belonged with her parents, but her heart said otherwise. It was going to be hard enough leaving her overnight at Rhonda's house, she couldn't imagine never seeing Abby again.

Despite her misgivings, Percy's presence calmed her. She noted his unfortunate gray pallor, wondering why he would choose clothes that mirrored that particular shade of dismal. Despite all the gray, he exuded a warmth that put Zoe at ease.

Percy walked straight to Abby, beaming. "Hello again, little one. How was your day today?"

Without hesitation, Abby looked up at Percy and launched into her own version of the day's events. It sounded like babble to everyone in the room, but Percy listened carefully and nodded his head.

"The playground, eh? And you had a pretzel? Three pretzels?"

Zoe leaned in to David. "How can he do that? How does he understand her?"

"I don't know," he whispered. "Some people are just good with kids, I guess."

Percy laughed at something Abby said before gesturing to the adults. "Why don't we go into the kitchen?" he suggested. "She wants to watch her television show out here."

As they all filed into the kitchen, Zoe looked back. Indeed, Abby was engrossed in an episode of *Wonder Pets*, content to stay in the living room.

Sitting around the large picnic table where meals were served in the kitchen, everyone stared expectantly at Percy. He cleared his throat before speaking. "First of all, you should know that every effort is being made to locate the parents. Unfortunately, it's not that easy. We have nothing to go on right now, so we're at a loss. The police want to release some of this information to the press to see if anyone comes forward."

Zoe tried to swallow past the lump in her throat.

"And what happens when you do find her parents?" David's voice was angry. "Do they get to just take her back? That doesn't seem like such a good option for Abby. Who deserts their kid in a mall, anyway?"

Percy nodded. "I know, I know, it's not a good situation. If the parents can be located then of course we would step in to assess the situation. But right now we're also looking at another possibility."

"I don't like the sound of this," Rhonda said.

"You're going to like it less when you hear this," Percy told them. "Last night police found evidence outside the mall that there may have been a crime committed." He hesitated, shifting with discomfort in his chair. "There was a large amount of blood found by a dumpster out back."

"Did they find a body?" Pete asked.

Percy shook his head. "No, not yet, but according to police whoever lost that amount of blood would be unlikely to survive. Now, remember, there may or may not be a connection between that and Abby, we won't know that for sure until we find out who got hurt back there. But it's possible that this little girl witnessed a crime that involved her parent or parents."

Zoe wrapped her arms around herself to stop from shivering. This was far from good news. "Is she in any danger?"

"We don't think so," Percy answered. "Nobody knows that she's here, and we think this is the safest place for her."

"We're going to be here as much as possible, so we'll be able to keep an eye on her," David was determined. "Nobody is going to get to her, not while I have anything to say about it."

Despite the situation, Rhonda grinned at her brother. "I've never seen you take such an interest in kids before."

David's eyes were grim. "This is different. Abby is family. I don't know how to explain it, but she is."

Zoe nodded. "That's right. Rhonda, if you don't mind, maybe we can set up a schedule so that we can spend more time with Abby. I don't want to get in your way, but I'd like to be here when I can."

Percy nodded. "That would be fine with me. Do you mean both of you, or just one of you?"

"Both of us," David and Zoe answered.

Percy smiled brightly at the group. "This is perfect, just perfect. Don't worry, everything is going to turn out exactly the way it's supposed to."

***

"You've had some crazy ideas before, but this one is beyond crazy. I think you need to take a step back and re-think this whole thing. I mean, this is your life you're talking about, right? And not just your life, but a child's life, too." Zoe was on her couch, listening as her friend Maggie's well-meaning voice came through the phone.

Staring at the lights on her Christmas tree, she answered. "Mags, I get that you're worried, I really do. If it were you, I'd be worried too. I just don't see any other way to do this."

Her cat jumped up to the window, eyeing the Christmas tree ornaments. There were so many holiday decorations for him to destroy, it was simply a question of what he was going to wreak havoc on next. Zoe picked up her *Seasons Greetings* throw pillow and launched it at the cat while she listened to Maggie. Not that it did any good to throw a pillow at a cat, but she had to try.

"Let's go over this again. You and David have gotten to know each other really well in the past few weeks, right?"

"Right." Although Maggie couldn't see it, Zoe blushed at the comment. The first night they had sex was burned into her memory as one of the most erotic moments of her lifetime. It didn't end there, either. It seemed they were always thinking up new ways to tantalize each other, ways that resulted in losing many nights of sleep.

"And you both care about this little girl who has no parents, right? Are the police positive there are no other relatives?"

Zoe remembered the night Percy delivered the news. Sitting at Rhonda's kitchen table, he sadly shook his head and told them Abby's mother had been murdered, her body found in the trunk of a car. The murderers had been caught, but Abby was without a mother.

"There was no father listed on the birth certificate, and the mother had no family to speak of. Percy put an ad in the paper looking for relatives, but no one has come forward. Percy moved pretty quickly to terminate parental rights, so even if there is a father out there he has no claim on her. Abby is legally available for adoption."

"Why don't you adopt her?" Maggie demanded.

Zoe hesitated. She knew that explaining this part would be difficult, but she had to try. "Percy told us that a judge was more likely to award custody to a married couple rather than a single person. He said that being married really helped in cases like this."

"He didn't mean you had to run out and get married right now!" Maggie exploded. "You haven't even known David that long, not long enough for a lifetime commitment, that's for sure."

Zoe knew her friend meant well. "Maggie, listen. This is different. I'm almost forty years old, I've dated a few men in my life. But this time I know, I really know, that David is the man I've been waiting for. There is no question in my mind that I want to spend the rest of my life with him, so this makes perfect sense to me."

"Does David know about this?"

Zoe hesitated. "No, not yet. I think he has the same feelings for me since he's told me he loves me, but I haven't discussed this with him yet."

"So your plan is to go over there tonight and ask him to marry you so you two can adopt Abby?"

Zoe grinned."Yep, that's the plan. Wish me luck."

Maggie sighed. "I have to say I envy you. I've never heard you talk about someone like this before, and I have no doubt you love him. I don't think you'll need luck, I think you already had luck when you found each other at the mall."

"Thanks, Maggie, that means a lot to me. I'll call you tomorrow and let you know what happens."

"Forget that. You better call me tonight, I don't care what time it is."

Zoe laughed. "Okay, it's a deal. Just don't yell at me when I wake you up."

***

Nothing ever goes according to plan. This was usually the case, but Zoe never had things go so wrong so fast. When she got to the house her excited anticipation quickly dropped to full blown dread.

As she climbed the front steps to Rhonda's house, David threw the door open. "Do you have Abby?"

"What? No, isn't she here?" David's words weren't making sense to Zoe.

"No, we can't find her and we've searched everywhere." David stood in the doorway, white faced and trembling. "She was outside on the swings one minute, gone the next. I only came inside for one second, to get her a juice box, and…"

37

"Have you called the police?" Zoe asked.

David nodded. "They're on their way."

Zoe couldn't take her eyes off David. This couldn't be happening, it just couldn't. Where could her baby be?

"Let's check the neighborhood."

"I've already done that, did you think I wouldn't look for her?" David's voice had an edge of hysteria.

Zoe took a deep breath. "I know you would've done that. Let's do it again. Sometimes kids hide."

David ran a hand through his hair, looking like he'd aged ten years in a day.

"Okay, we'll split up."

Zoe heard the sirens. Thank God, help would be here soon.

"Let them know we're out looking," Zoe said to Rhonda, who was standing behind David. She took off at a sprint across the yard, yelling for Abby.

Zoe stopped after a few minutes, trying to ignore the panic that was building. If she were Abby, where would she go and why would she hide? Zoe could hear David's voice in the distance. He'd gone the opposite way, trying to cover as much ground as possible. She could see the uniformed patrolmen knocking on neighbor's doors. Hopefully someone knew something.

Crossing through a yard to get to a parallel street, Zoe hesitated. It was probably a waste of time to keep searching the neighborhood. David and the police would take care of this area. Turning and running back to her car, Zoe clutched her keys and prayed. *Let me find her.*

***

The mall was only a few miles from Rhonda's house. It was hard to believe only a few weeks ago she hadn't known Abby or David. Now, she didn't want to live without either of them. Stepping out of the car, she scanned the parking lot and tried to remember what Percy had said. *Abby's mother was murdered and left in the trunk of a car. Had she been murdered inside the mall, or outside, and why was she killed?*

Zoe shivered, wondering if whoever did this to Abby's mother was looking for Abby. Could the little girl have seen something?

Slamming her car door, she began to half-jog past the rows of cars. Zoe's plan was to check the entire parking area before going into the mall. Increasing her speed,, she ignored the knot of pain settling in her stomach. Something was very wrong, and Zoe could almost hear the ticking of a clock, telling her she was running out of time.

It took ten achingly long minutes before she spotted the dark sedan parked at the edge of the lot. In that moment, Zoe knew. "Abby," she whispered, and began to run.

***

David didn't know what the hell Zoe was doing, but he trusted her. Seeing her run to her car and tear out of the driveway, he grabbed Officer Randall, the police officer standing next to him.

"She knows something, let's go."

When there's a missing child, nobody hesitates. With David in the front seat of the patrol car, the officer radioed for backup.

"She's going to the mall," David muttered.

"Why would she do that?" Officer Randall asked.

"It's where we found her. The little girl."

"Is this the kid whose mother got killed here?"

David nodded grimly. "Yeah."

"Damn. I hope your girlfriend's wrong about this."

David stared out the window, trying to control his emotions. "Me too."

As the car circled the parking lot, the two men strained to look through the rows of parked vehicles.

Zoe, where are you? Where's Abby?

"There, she's right there…," David shouted, pointing to the dark car that Zoe was running toward.

Jumping out before Officer Randall could come to a complete stop, David broke into a run.

A moment later, he heard it. Gunshots.

***

David wondered if he was having a reaction to recent events. Almost losing Abby and Zoe had made him realize what was truly important. When the gun had fired, he'd gone a little crazy. Events in his mind were still foggy, but the one thing he clearly remembered was tackling the thug with the gun.

David paced up and down Rhonda's kitchen. "What if I'm wrong? What if this is a really bad idea?"

Rhonda stood and put a hand on his shoulder. "For heaven's sake, sit down already, you're wearing a hole in the floor. Why would this be such a bad idea?"

David hesitated. "Maybe I'm having some sort of post-traumatic stress reaction. Everything seems so perfect, almost too perfect."

Rhonda laughed. "Don't worry, that will go away with time."

"It will?"

"Sure it will. There's going to come a point where you two annoy each other, or she yells at you for leaving your socks on the floor, or you wonder why she didn't have time to do laundry when she was home all day. The perfect part doesn't last forever, but the other part does."

"What other part?"

"The friend part. Knowing that the person you married is your best friend and you can tell them anything. Feeling like you have someone in your life you can count on, someone who will listen to you, that's the other part. Pete and I might fight about dishes left in the sink, but at the end of the day he's the person I tell my secrets to."

David stared at his sister for a moment. "You know, I never really gave you guys enough credit, and I'm sorry for that. All I ever saw was what your house looked like, or I couldn't understand why you wouldn't let me buy you things. You don't need things, do you? I'm so sorry for all those times I acted like an ass."

Rhonda hugged her brother. "Don't worry about it, you're family and I love you anyway. But now that you've seen the light, maybe I'll let you buy me a new living room set."

The sound of the doorbell stopped him from answering her. From the kitchen, he could hear Pete letting Zoe in the house. At the sound of Zoe's voice, Abby ran into the kitchen, hands waving in the air to be picked up and a smile on her face.

"Well, look who's up from her nap," Rhonda exclaimed. "Let me just get you cleaned up a little –"

"No," David interrupted. "I can't stand it much longer, I can't wait. I would really like her to be here for this."

"Be here for what?" Zoe asked, walking into the kitchen.

Rhonda looked at Zoe, worried. "How are you feeling?"

"Fine, it was nothing. The bullet barely scratched my skin." Zoe shuddered. "I just can't bear to think about –"

"Don't," David interrupted. "The worst is over. They're gone."

"What if –"

"No 'what ifs'," David was adamant. "The stolen drugs were recovered, nobody has any reason to look for us or Abby anymore."

"I still don't understand why they thought they had to take Abby," Rhonda said, shaking her head. "For goodness sake, she's not even two years old. She still can't speak in complete sentences yet."

"Another smart criminal," Zoe said drily. "The world's full of them."

David hastened to reassure everyone. "The police issued a very public statement about the whole thing, and they have no reason to bother us anymore. Plus, everyone connected to this thing is in jail. We're safe."

Zoe shuddered. "For now. Hey, what's Abby supposed to be here for?"

David cleared his throat. "Zoe, you know that you and Abby mean the world to me –"

"Mama." Abby squirmed, eyes big, and reached out to Zoe.

"Oh, sweetheart," Zoe's eyes filled with tears as she scooped the child into her arms.

"Dada." This time Abby was looking straight at David.

Laughing, he nodded. "That's right, Abby, that's what I'm trying to do." Getting down on one knee, he looked up at Zoe.

"Zoe Dearborn, will you marry me?"

There was a silence in the kitchen as Zoe stood there, trying to catch her breath. Finally, unable to stand it any longer, she answered.

"Yes."

"Yes," Abby echoed, looking at Zoe.

"And of course we're going to apply to adopt you, sweetheart," David told the little girl, standing and circling his arms around both his girls.

"I don't think that will be a problem at all," Percy's voice boomed through the kitchen.

"Percy, when did you get here?" Rhonda asked.

"Oh, I've been watching for a while now," the social worker answered. "And I couldn't think of a better ending than this one. Will you have a Christmas wedding?"

Zoe smiled. "I think that would be perfect. A simple Christmas wedding."

David frowned at Zoe. "There's just… I'm sorry, things have been so crazy I didn't get you a ring, and I wasn't sure what you wanted…"

"David, I've gotten exactly what I wanted, don't worry."

"And what is that, young lady?" Percy asked.

"I've gotten a family for Christmas," Zoe answered.

***

The strains of a soft melody could be heard as the last of the holiday workers filed into the clearing. The faint light of dawn had just started to wake into the space, revealing row after row of the gray people. Some could barely be seen as their image shimmered in the soft light. There was an excitement in the air at the possibilities in this post-Christmas meeting.

"Okay, everybody, okay, let's get started," Gabe called. "First of all, I want to say to all of you, excellent work this year, excellent. We had an extremely successful program again, and that's because of your hard work. From the list I have, it looks like I'll be taking some of you back with me this year. Now, let's talk about what happened."

"I have to say, I always enjoy the chance we're given to redeem ourselves. I know I wasted a lifetime through my indifference, but I'm starting to feel like I might be making up for that," Percy said. "This assignment was especially touching, too."

Gabe nodded. "Yes, earth is a marvelous place. Now tell me, you had the orphaned girl and the couple, right?"

"Yes. So sad that the mother had to leave her daughter, but obviously it was for the best. The mother died in a drug deal gone bad, and that is no way to raise a child."

"She's with us, now, and she's recovering nicely," Gabe's assistant, Cleo, piped in from the other side of the room. "Lovely woman, really, I think she just lost her way."

Most of the gray figures in the room nodded, being all too familiar with the ways that the humans got lost. After all, they themselves had once been human. Lifetimes lived without caring, days slipping by without purpose, it all added up to an afterlife of in-between. These were the ones that hovered, the beings that were not yet allowed to cross over after death. Their purpose now was to make up for all that. Some, like Percy, were diligent in making amends. Although he could've moved on, Percy chose to remain earthbound. The joy in helping others was too much for him to resist, and he found a satisfaction in these assignments he'd never achieved during his human life.

Others wandered, still lost.

"It's a good thing those folks didn't know much about the law, though," Percy added. "There were a few times I had to sort of stretch things to make everything work out the way it was supposed to."

"You didn't break the rules, did you?" Gabe asked, frowning.

"No, of course not, I just spent some time convincing judges and agencies to do things a certain way, that's all. No rules were broken."

"Good."

Percy sighed. "I was especially glad they got this child as it seems Zoe won't be having any others."

"What makes you say that?" Gabe demanded.

"She said she was too old to bear children."

Gabe let loose with a laugh. "Humans are so funny. They have these ideas of what their lives are going to be like, and they never seem to get it right."

"You mean that's not true?" Percy asked, hopeful. David and Zoe were so good with the child, it would be a shame if they didn't have more.

"No, it's not true," Gabe answered. "In fact, let me see…" Consulting a clipboard in his hand, he looked up at Percy. "We've got a birth scheduled to Zoe in August of their time. In fact, oh my… It looks like you're going to have quite an interesting assignment with those two in a few years, Percy."

Percy was confused. "A few years? What could possibly be happening by then?"

"Twins."

A Soul for Christmas

A Tale from the Crossroads

By

Jackie Guidry

Merry Christmas. Hope you enjoy the book.

Jackie Guidry

Mahlah pressed against the damp, rough cabin wall and eavesdropped on her Papa. He was speaking to a large, ruddy stranger. As a woman of eight and ten years, Mahlah could not forgive her own spying, especially on Christmas Eve, but the feeling in her gut would not go away. Dark superstitions about the location of their new home and church did not encourage the usual Christmas spirit either. Perhaps her unease stemmed from that.

Would every passerby drive their animals through the church's muddy front yard instead of the crossing roads before them?

Wisps of cloves, cinnamon, and cranberries from her mother's cooking wafted outside the cabin. Mahlah's stomach gurgled. She pressed the egg basket against her stomach and watched her father, the Parson Pritchard, drag mother's Christmas greens over to the ruddy stranger's wagon. Mother would not be happy about that. She would forgive him though, knowing he did it for the sake of God and their greater calling.

The two men shoved the thick evergreen branches under the stranger's mud- bogged mule cart. Pine planks would have made a better choice but her Papa wanted to discourage the superstitious offenders, not give them easy passage.

Mahlah's damp skirts clung to her clammy legs but she kept still, waiting to hear if this stranger believed in a devil at the crossroads like everyone else. Their new home was an odd place. The two dirt roads that separated the four towns lay in front of their new cabin. The north, south, east and west running roads met in a visually ordinary, yet prefect cross. Neither bird nor beast willingly traveled across the intersecting roads in front of the cabin, but Mahlah theorized a scientific reason, not a mystical one. Too bad the locals believed in the opposite, though. Even the lumberyard employees refused to deliver lumber for the new church building.

The Bishop thought that if a parson and his family resided at the crossroads, the locals would stop accusing each other of making deals with the devil who operated there. Mahlah sighed then stared at the indentation in the very center of the crossroads. If only the Bishop could see her now, he would see that she was a traitor to all Christmas stood for. What type of young woman had a head full of devils and spied on her Papa while her mother prepared the Christmas feast alone?

Her Papa handed the stranger a rake.

"If we want to get you home for Christmas," her Papa said, "I think we best rake some of these wheel ruts out, then scatter more branches so you can circle back to the road."

The stranger's face paled as he shook his head, "Now see here Parson," he huffed, "I know you're new around these parts, an' I beg your pardon, but, these here mules ain't gonna take kindly to that idea. They's already spooked on accounts of that panther I shot back there."

Her Papa narrowed his eyes, "A panther? I did not think many survived off Virginia's Chesapeake Bay here."

"Ha! That beast's bin stalk'n us for months now so, I ain't rattling them mules no more than need be. If my woman wasn't need'n this medicine," he patted his coat pocket, "I'd a never chanced going into New Hayes."

Her Papa shook his head then leaned on the rake. "A panther you say? Are you certain?"

"Sure as we're standing here now." The stranger pointed the rake back toward the town of New Hayes. "Your neighbor saw the whole thing, Damn beast jumped out of that low oak on the edge of his field, near that bend in the road."

The stranger slid the hat off his head, covered his heart and looked to the sky. "I thank the Almighty for make'n me a good shot though. I think I grazed his shoulder but he took off before I could end him." He returned his hat to his head and spit in the mud. "It's the third time in as many months he's gotten the drop on me, too."

The hair on Mahlah's neck stood up. Slowly, her eyes swept the shadowy tree line. Just before the stranger arrived, her older brother Robert had headed out in those woods to hunt up kindling wood. She prayed that the stranger was mistaken, then prayed that Robert would hurry home safe. The Christmas of 1821 was turning out to be the eeriest Christmas on record for her.

Again, she turned and surveyed the haunting woods. Could she make it back into the cabin without her Papa noticing? Surely not, she could only watch while she waited. Her Papa's shoulders slouched and he looked tired, wet and weary,

"Alright, alright," he said to the stranger. "If you and your mules insist on this path, it is your choice."

While tamping some mud into the deep wheel ruts, her Papa bit his bottom lip. With a twinkle in his eye, he stopped and looked up.

"How 'bout I make a deal with you and your mules?"

"A deal?" The stranger cocked back his head and waved his hands in front of him. "Ah-ah, Parson. Nobody 'round here makes deals this close to the," he nodded toward the crossroads then whispered, "you know what."

Her Papa rolled his eyes and the stranger said, "Not that I believe in such nonsense, mind you. It's just, old traditions die hard, you see."

She suppressed a giggle. If her Papa thought he could convince this man to abandon his superstitions and return to the road, he sure had his work cut out for him.

Her Papa said, "Alright, we won't call it a deal then." He dug his rake back into the ground and added, "It was only a figure of speech anyhow. It's a shame to forfeit the reward, though."

The stranger's eyebrow went up. "Not a deal you say? Well, if there is a reward, let us hear it."

Wondering if the 'us' the stranger kept mentioning included his mules, Mahlah waited to hear more. Her Papa stopped pushing around the mud, looked up and leaned on his rake again. Starting at the man's thick brow and moving his eyes down the stranger's tree trunk-like foundation, her Papa seemed to be taking measure of the stranger.

Her Papa paused then shook his head in disappointment.

"Nah, maybe not…"

The stranger's mouth hung open then shut tight. He held his chin high and looked down his nose at her Papa.

"Well if you are too afraid to speak of it… then that's that."

Mahlah knew her Papa's strategy well. He used it on her older brother, Robert, all of the time. Her Papa wrinkled his brow and scratched his beard.

"Now hold on. I could have you pegged wrong, friend."

The stranger folded his thick arms across his chest, his pride blazed in his nostrils.

"I'm sure you have," said the stranger, then he spit into the mud again.

Her Papa shrugged, "Well, it is the eve of our savior's birth. And the day is growing short. Maybe you are not so foolish as to miss this rare challenge and reap the rewards."

After pondering, the stranger rubbed his wife's medicine bulging in his worn coat pocket, and then answered.

"T'ain't no man can say I ever shied away from proving my grit." He kept his hand over his pocket this time, cleared his throat and asked, "Did you say, reward?"

A clatter near the barn frightened Mahlah. She stumbled forward, out into the open and almost dropped the egg basket. Her heart pounded as the stranger yanked his rifle off the mule cart and aimed at the commotion. As the sleek figure stepped away from the barn and into the light, Mahlah screamed.

"Robert!"

The stranger swung his rifle in her direction. As she covered her face, her Papa raised his forearm. With little force, he bumped the stranger's barrel and altered the riffles line of fire at the woods instead of her chest. The stranger panted.

In a firm voice her Papa said, "It's not your panther friend, it is my children."

The cabin's front door flew open and Mother yelled, "Mahlah? Did you holler for me?"

Mother's eyes focused on the scene before her. Her slender hand clutched the doorframe and she gasped. After following the direction the rifle pointed, her mother screamed.

"Mahlah!"

In a barrage of Christmas aromas, her mother leapt off the steps and wrapped her arms around her. They held each other while her Papa pulled the rifle from the stranger.

"Dear God. Dear God..." chanted the stranger.

Robert ran up beside him.

"Father!"

Her Papa sat the rifle on the mule cart. "It's alright, son. Our friend here has had a run-in with a panther and thought the beast might be trailing him."

Mother glanced at Mahlah and Mahlah shrugged. Maybe, in the commotion, no one realized she had been eavesdropping.

*****

When the stranger comprehended he had almost shot the parson's children, his face turned a greenish hue. Alarmed at the way the stranger swayed, Mother and Robert led him to the log bench by the stairs. Expressionless, he plopped down and the bench groaned.

"Mahlah," said her mother, "get Mr…" Mother paused, realizing she did not know the stranger's name.

The man twitched and the color ran back into his face. He looked up at her mother.

"Ham Bone," he said. "They call me Ham Bone Magee."

Mother smiled reassuringly, "Get Mr. Ha… um, Mr. Magee, a mug of the spiced tea."

"Folks just calls me Ham Bone, Ma'am." Unblinking, Ham Bone glanced at Mahlah, then Robert and said, "I could have killed you both…"

Mother patted his filthy hand, "But you didn't. Mahlah, obviously Mr. Ma… I mean, Mr. Ham Bone, is in need of some warm Christmas hospitality and we have disappointed. Hurry now."

"Yes Mother," said Mahlah.

When she returned with the aromatic tea, her Papa and Robert had the stranger's mules trudging back toward the road. Fish belly white replaced the green in Ham Bone's face but

53

Mahlah could not tell if it was an improvement in his countenance or not. At least he sat upright and straight-faced. The change in his demeanor and the direction of the mules convinced Mahlah that her Papa had succeeded. Mr. Ham Bone had decided to attempt the crossroads.

He took the mug in his thick hand while watching his mules.

"Do you feel that?" he asked to no one in particular.

Her Papa stopped yanking the mule's harness, narrowed his eyes and asked, "Feel what, friend?"

Ham Bone pivoted his head from left to right, scanning their surroundings.

"As if the hair on your neck is standing at attention." He leaned forward and said, "As if ice is riding through your veins, shouting that your death is watching, and waiting."

Mahlah hugged herself and shivered. The four family members exchanged questioning glances. Mother moved away from Mr. Ham Bone and sidled over to Mahlah.

Her Papa patted one of the mules on the neck and said, "I believe we all feel that way at some point in our lives. The trick is to remember the Lord walks beside us through all our earthly trials and that every path will lead to Him."

As if fueled by Ham Bone's unease, the mules twitched and jerked their heads up and down. Robert and her Papa held tight as the mules trudged forward, freeing themselves and the cart from the mud without encouragement. Wide eyed, Ham Bone stood as Robert hopped up onto the cart and steadied the reins.

"Whoa, whoa."

Mr. Ham Bone handed the mug to her mother then headed toward the cart.

"Duke, Duchess…" he said. " I know, I know." He grabbed the rifle off the cart and studied the trees. "I feel him, too."

Her mother and Papa's eyes met. Papa's eyes telegraphed regret while Mother's conveyed fear. Mahlah stood still, wondering who the "he" was. She kept an eye on the rifle, and wondered why her Papa had not held on to it. Even though Ham Bone seemed unnerved, he placed a hand on Duchess's neck, whispered something, and she stopped stomping. A moment later, Duke followed suit.

"Robert? Give the reins over to Mr. Ham Bone and go saddle my horse."

Mr. Ham Bone took a deep breath, "I didn't know you was in a hurry, Parson. As soon as you do what you promised, I'll be on my way."

"You have not kept me." Her Papa smiled and looked into Mother's eyes. "You have convinced me to see you home safe."

"And to keep an eye out for the panther?"

"That's right," said Papa as he steadied the mules while Mr. Ham Bone mounted the cart. "All the way."

Not only did Mr. Ham Bone's face crack into a toothless smile, he stroked the rifle in his lap. Robert glanced at the rifle then looked Ham Bone up and down as if he had just come across an ogre under a bridge.

"I'll go with you." Robert said. He raised his collar and strode toward the barn. Her Papa yelled.

"Not today, Son." Robert stopped and her Papa said, "You stay here."

The mules snorted and pranced back and forth. Her Papa looked around and nodded towards the cabin. "Mahlah, get the shotgun for your brother. Neither of you two had better come out of the cabin without Robert and the shotgun while I'm gone. If our friend is correct, that panther could mean trouble."

Mahlah rushed over and took her Papa's hands. "Don't go, Papa. It's Christmas Eve and Robert is only home from the Seminary for a short while. Besides, it gets dark early now. It will be dark before you can head home."

Her Papa patted her hand and said, "Now, now, enough of that. Hurry and bring the shotgun and ammunition for your brother."

Jealousy, fear and loneliness churned in Mahlah's gut. Why did this stranger have to ruin their Christmas? She swallowed to hold back her frustration and the forlorn feelings growing inside her. If she told Papa about her uneasy feelings, he would only laugh and blame their odd new surroundings and their lack of holiday party invitations.

Something cold and damp dripped onto her cheek. Soft plopping noises followed as the drizzle hit the fallen leaves. Papa lifted his own collar and turned to talk with her mother. Again, Mahlah pivoted and entered the cabin alone.

Cramped was the only way to describe the cabin. The main room served as a kitchen, living room and study all rolled into one. The three separate bedrooms tucked into the left side of the cabin, and their books were the only luxuries. Baked goods lay cooling on the kitchen table and the smell announced that Christmas was here. Her stomach gurgled again but she paid it no mind.

At the primitive fireplace mantel, she reached for the mounted shotgun and japanned ammunition tin. Red and orange embers glowed in the fireplace, but she did not dare waste time warming herself. Time was in short supply.

Exiting the cabin, she found Papa standing over Mr. Ham Bone's bowed head, reciting a prayer.

"...in your name we humbly ask. Amen."

Mother and Robert repeated, "Amen."

Robert strode over and snatched the gun and ammunition tin from her. Even though he was almost a preacher himself, he still took pleasure in taunting her. With his back turned to the others, he rolled his eyes then prepared the shotgun for duty.

"You said you was going to bless my mules too, Preacher."

Papa nodded and circled around to the mules. He placed his hands on their noses, and then bowed his head. Robert nudged Mahlah's ribs and they both bowed their own heads, even though she did not feel like it.

"Lord, protect these loyal mules, Duke and, and…"

Mr. Ham Bone looked up and whispered, "Duchess…Duke and Duchess."

Papa nodded "Yes, Duchess. Lord, on this, the eve of your son's birth, protect and watch over Duke and Duchess. Keep these loyal beasts of burden safe from all evils and help them to help their master serve in your cause. This we humbly ask in your holy name. Amen."

They repeated, "Amen."

Mahlah leaned in and whispered to Robert, "What's that about?"

Robert grinned, shook his head and whispered back, "Papa promised that if he blessed the man and his mules, no evil would follow them home from the crossroads. That in the next life,, he'd be rewarded for this act of faith."

"And he's going for it?"

Mahlah and Robert glanced at Mr. Ham Bone, grinning like a babe with sweets.

Robert shrugged, "I guess. He could still fold though. Or get nervous and shoot somebody."

Robert handed the tin back to her, winked then strode toward the barn. The drizzle ceased as Mother moved past her, and hurried into the cabin. Mahlah was about to follow but halted when Mr. Ham Bone spoke.

"Do blessings work even if the person hasn't done right?"

Her Papa leaned against the cart and said, "Well, if the person is truly sorry and asks forgiveness from God, then strives to never do that thing again. Then, yes. But at the same time we must remember that our wants are not always the Lord's needs."

Mr. Ham Bone paused then glanced at Mahlah.

"Can we speak without...?"

He tilted his head toward Mahlah and her face warmed. Papa turned.

"Mahlah, I believe you have something to do?"

Mahlah tripped over her feet, embarrassed that Papa had to ask. Inside the cabin, she heard Mother rustling around in the bedroom. She poked the embers in the fireplace then added a log. In normal circumstances, she would never think twice about Papa's discussions with parishioners, but tonight her curiosity would not let up.

She removed her coat and walked to her room. Hanging it on the peg by the window, Mahlah heard Papa's voice. When she leaned against the shudder, Mr. Ham Bone spoke.

"We were told he drowned at the mouth of the Chesapeake during a squall. We even waited before we married but he was my best friend and deep down, I think I always knew."

"Knew what?"

"Knew he was alive, washed up somewhere… Shoot, preacher, I thought everybody knew this story 'round these parts."

Her Papa paused, then said, "I guess we would have, but, we were so busy with the yellow fever outbreak when we arrived…"

"Well," Mr. Ham Bone said, "when Lucy opened the front door, I 'bout fell off my chair. Lucy was hugging and crying on him with my child in her belly. It was as if my heart had been ripped from my chest."

"That is understandable. Any man would feel that."

"True. But, when he noticed her swollen belly, he changed. He started calling Lucy a whore, and worse, so… I hit him."

"I see."

"Parson, Earl's a tough, wiry son of a…" Mr. Ham Bone paused, and then said, "Sorry Parson. I mean, I knocked him flat, then he stood back up but I hit him again, so hard, he tumbled out the door and into the street."

Mahlah scratched her leg and wondered if she would have done the same thing if she were a man in his situation.

"Is that all?"

"No, Parson. When the neighbors and a few drunks gathered around, Earl didn't let up. He started …"

"Mahlah?"

Mother pushed the bedroom door wide and Mahlah jumped.

"What are you doing?"

"I, um…"

"Are you eavesdropping on your father?" Mother's eyes widened, "And on Christmas Eve…"

Mahlah squeezed her thumb and said, "I, I…" Mother scowled and she knew she could not lie, "Oh, all right. Yes. You caught me."

Mother tsk-tsked.

"I know I shouldn't but I have a horrible…" Mahlah stopped talking when her words triggered worry in her mother's eyes.

"A horrible what?"

Mahlah swallowed. She did not want to worry Mother more, so she said, "A horrible curiosity."

*****

The men stopped talking when Mahlah and her mother exited the cabin. Guilty for listening to their conversation, she avoided their eyes and looked up. The downy clouds had unfurrowed above them. Now, the patches were one thick, grey blanket, stretching to the horizon. Mother looked up also, pulling her shawl tight while shivering.

Her Papa turned to Mr. Ham Bone and said, "Give us a moment, will you?"

Mr. Ham Bone tipped his hat to her and her Mother and said, "By all means. I'll roll the wheels a bit to knock loose the mud, then scrape our hooves."

Before the crossroads, he circled back toward New Hayes. When he rolled out of earshot, Mother shoved her Papa's slicker and food into Mahlah's arms and grabbed her Papa's hands.

"I don't want you going with that man. He is too jumpy with that gun. He almost shot our children."

Surprised by her mother's reaction, Mahlah quickly nodded her agreement. Her Papa clasped one of Mahlah's hands and squeezed one of Mother's.

"That is why I need to see him home. How could we live with ourselves, if tomorrow, on Christmas morn, someone comes to the door to say that I have to bury a loved one he accidently shot?"

Mahlah and Mother both looked at each other then dropped their eyes as her Papa continued.

"Christmas Eve is a night of neighbors visiting neighbors. There will be too many chances for our friend to stumble across someone. And after what I have just heard from his own lips, he truly believes he is being stalked by a panther and he is," her Papa paused, and then said, "he is impulsive."

Mention of a man stalking panther did not shock Mahlah as much as it did her mother but she still had a hard time believing it. Large cold raindrops splattered here and there when Robert emerged from the barn with the mare. Mother took the slicker from Mahlah and helped her Papa into it. She opened the leather satchel and pointed out the contents.

"There are some dried apples, venison jerky and a bit of brandy to keep you warm. Not too much mind you."

Her Papa nodded, "Thank you, dear."

Robert approached and steadied the horse. He nudged her Papa in the back with an elbow, then held out the shotgun.

"Here," Robert said, "for warding off panthers." He nodded toward Mr. Ham Bone, rolled his eyes and mumbled, "And other things."

Her Papa shook his head, but Robert insisted. "We have grandfather's pistol here. And besides, I plan on staying in the cabin and catching up on my theology. So don't you dare leave me home for long with these two. They'll be imagining you defenseless, with a panther picking his teeth with your bones."

Mother smacked his arm, "Robert! That is, that…"

"Oh Mother, there's no panther." He rubbed his arm, grinned and said, "See Father, they're already falling to pieces…"

Her Papa gave a little smile and took the shotgun. "Alright."

Robert and Mahlah both hugged Papa and Robert winked at her behind his back. Apparently, both men had strategies for dealing with each other. Slipping on his gloves, her Papa hollered that he was ready.

As Mr. Ham Bone pulled the mule cart around, her Papa whispered, "If anyone else comes through here, best mention the panther. I'll stop by the Sherriff's and see what he has to say about our friend's peculiar behavior."

The mare stared wide-eyed at the crossroads. There was no way that the animal wanted to go anywhere near that intersection.

"Papa," she said, "do you think this is the best time to encourage our rifle-baring friend to take on his superstitions?"

Her Papa shrugged, "I can't discourage him now. It might only strengthen his belief." Her Papa smiled, "Don't worry, faith will see us through."

"Robert," said her Papa as they all watched Mr. Ham Bone stroke his rifle again, "I promised our friend that I'd guide his mules through the crossroads, so I want you to bring our mare through."

After shrugging, Robert swung up into the saddle. She wished she could move as fluidly.

"Now remember," her Papa said as he climbed into the cart, "don't underestimate her, and stay clear of these mules."

Mahlah squeezed her mother's hands. How the animals would react was no secret and by the looks of things, Mr. Ham Bone still felt the same way. He shifted his weight and lowered a foot to the ground. Her Papa grabbed his coat sleeve.

"Hold on a minute friend. I said I would drive the cart if you promised to stay in it."

Ham Bone slid back on to the seat and asked, "Are you sure I'm blessed? Even after what I told you earlier?"

Her Papa patted Ham Bone's knee, "It is our faith that blesses us and keeps us safe. Lose that and you have bigger things to worry about than these crossroads. Besides, it is our Savior's Birthday. Going through this intersection will be a great gift of faith to Him. Can't you feel Him watching us…?"

As if he were basking in the sun, her Papa closed his eyes and tilted his face to the sky. Mr. Ham Bone cocked his head back in disbelief. Her Papa opened his eyes and nudged him.

"Go ahead," he said. "Try it. Let yourself feel His presence."

With their eyes shut, the two threw back their heads in silence. Mahlah could not help smirking with Robert, but her mother put a finger to her lips and they both resumed their straight faces.

"You see?" her Papa asked as he opened his eyes. "Did you feel His grace welling up inside you?"

Mr. Ham Bone pondered then said, "I felt something, but," he rubbed his belly, "I think it was just gas."

Her Papa hung his head and chuckled. "Well," he said as he flicked the reins, "here we go."

*****

Mr. Ham Bone squeezed his rifle as her Papa urged the mule cart to the infamous crossroads. Duke the mule whinnied and flung his tale in circles, but Duchess paid no mind to him. As the mules stepped into the crossroads, her mother winced and Mahlah held her breath. The mules ears laid flat but they turned toward Grouper Town without incident.

Her mother's mouth gaped open and then she said, "Well I'll be."

Grinning from ear to ear, her Papa halted the cart and patted Mr. Ham Bone on the back. Mr. Ham Bone wiped his brow, rested his face in his hands then looked up and said, "It worked! Your blessing really worked!"

Mahlah could not be certain but it sounded like he was repeating, "Thank you Jesus, thank you Jesus…"

Even Robert looked impressed then her Papa hollered to him, "Now Robert, remember what I said about bringing her through…"

Robert rolled his eyes and nudged the sorrel in the sides with his heels.

"Yes, sir."

The mare sidestepped through the mud, stepped onto the road, then stopped. The sorrel's ears went back and she tossed her head. Robert petted her neck and whispered.

"Come on now, don't embarrass us…"

Mahlah squeezed her mother's hands as Robert nudged the horse's sides with his heels again. The horse's tail spun and her head nodded but she did not move. Harder, he kicked, but, nothing. Robert groaned and swung down from the saddle. As he yanked the horse's bridle, she reared up, almost jerking him off the ground.

Her mother screamed, "Robert!"

Mahlah struggled to hold her back. A moment later, Robert had the mare at the cusp of the crossroads, pulling with all his might.

"Careful, son," yelled her Papa.

To everyone's surprise, Robert hopped back into the saddle, startling the mare across the intersection with three hops. Mr. Ham Bone shook his head.

"If I didn't know better," he said, "I'd think you forgot to bless your own horse, Parson."

Robert and her Papa exchanged glances but did not say a word. After straddling the mare, and securing the shotgun, her Papa hollered, "I'll see you a few hours after dark."

While waving, the two men disappeared into the misty rain beyond the crossroads. On Robert's walk back to Mahlah and her mother, he kicked a rock, stopped, and then kicked another one. Mahlah knew he did not want to face their worries so she brought up the one subject Robert could not resist.

"Do you think Lorna Gudmund would like to borrow my copy of Shakespeare?"

Surprised, Robert looked up. After studying her face, he quickly dropped his eyes again. He knocked his muddy boots against the boot scraper next to the steps.

"How should I know what Ms. Gudmund would like? I mean, if you enjoyed it, I am sure your friend will enjoy it also."

Her mother nudged her in the arm, shooting a reproachful look at her before heading inside. Mahlah waited under the cabin overhang to help Robert remove his muddy boots. She so wanted to ask him if he and her only local friend, Lorna Gudmund had exchanged letters or not. He probably would not answer her, though. She leaned inside the cabin, but before she could ask her mother if she needed more wood, Robert looked up.

"How is Lorna's brother, Vikar doing?" Robert grinned and asked, "Does he like to read Shakespeare?"

Mahlah felt her face warm but she hoped Robert could not see.

"He is well," she said, "although, I could not guess at what he likes or thinks. Papa says their smoked and salted fish business is profiting, and Lorna told me people are not shunning them socially, as often."

Robert nodded as he stomped his feet, looking relieved.

"Good. These people are so backwards in their beliefs… You know, it's usually the guilty ones that are busy pointing fingers…"

Mahlah pulled her shawl tighter, "I know. And so does Vikar and Lorna."

Robert sat on the threshold and stuck his foot in the air.

"Ah ha!" he said. "You do speak to Vikar."

She yanked off his boot then kicked his thigh.

"Of course I do, silly." She yanked off the second boot. "I am his sister's best friend. I also help with the children when they need me."

After the yellow fever outbreak killed their parents, Vikar, the eldest Gudmund, and his twin sister Lorna took responsibility for their five younger siblings. Luckily, they found a way to make a tidy profit selling smoked and salted fish to the yellow fever outbreak survivors. Since most folks missed the opportunity to stock up on other staples for the winter, business was booming and the children would have a plentiful Christmas.

Her Papa said that Vikar not only had a strong back and commanding presence, he had a good heart and a head for business. Too bad the locals suspected the Gudmunds of dark deals at the crossroads. Briefly, she wondered how life would be if she and Robert married the twins. Would they have to split up the five younger siblings or would one couple keep all five?

Still smirking, Robert picked up his boots and they walked into the cabin. The warm fire and the smell of the spiced baked goods made her miss her Papa and feel sorry for him. As they peeled off their first damp layer, her mother came out of her bedroom.

"Did you bring in firewood?"

Mahlah and Robert stopped peeling clothing and glanced at each other. Then, Mahlah shrugged her shawl back on.

"You already have your boots off," Mahlah said. "I'll go."

As she walked back to the door, her mother caught her sleeve.

"Wait."

With a determined look, her mother pulled grandfathers old pistol from her apron pocket. Mahlah wondered how deep those pockets were until her mother handed her the firearm. The weight led her to believe they were not only deep but also reinforced.

"Can you carry this and the wood?"

Mahlah did not know what to say. She supposed she could. Although, if she would actually shoot something was the question her mother should have asked. Doubt must have shown in her face because her mother shook her head then swatted her hand in the air.

"Never mind. Go warm yourself." Her mother took back the pistol. "Just open the door when I come back."

Before Robert could get to his feet, or Mahlah could protest, her mother strode out the door.

Robert threw a damp sock at her. "Go on, go help her!"

"Right."

Embarrassed, Mahlah hurried toward the lean-to covered woodpile. It was hard to believe that the old pistol would fire, let alone stop a panther. Of course, she did not believe there was a panther. Did the Sherriff know that Mr. Ham Bone believed a panther stalked him? He did mention that their neighbor saw the panther, though. Perhaps Robert could go and verify Mr. Ham Bone's story.

Her mother smiled when she saw her then glanced at the sky.

"It's getting darker already. How 'bout you carry and I load?"

Breathless, Mahlah nodded.

As her mother placed a large log in her arms, the wind shook the water off the wet trees. Large cold droplets pattered on the leaf-covered ground, sounding like tiny drums. Using her shoulder, she mopped up the ones that hit her cheek. With her head turned, her eye caught a large shadowy figure skulking up the road. She paused, focused, but could not make the figure out though the grey haze and drizzle.

Too busy looking for dry logs, her mother did not notice the figure. Mahlah nudged her.

"Mother," she whispered, even though the figure was still too far away to hear.

Her mother turned and Mahlah pointed past the cemetery, toward New Hayes. The dark mass slowly zigzagged toward them. It looked like a mound one moment, then a slender man the next. Her mother stacked another log in her arms.

"Go get your brother."

As Mahlah carried the logs toward the cabin, the figure stumbled off the opposite side of the road and disappeared. Mahlah's heart pounded. It looked like a man, but she could not say for certain. She ran up the steps and kicked at the door.

"Robert, Robert!"

The door opened. Robert blocked her entrance and said, "Patience is a virtue, Mahlah…" He looked around and over her, then poked his head out. "Where's Mother?"

Mahlah dropped the logs on the floor, just missing the moccasins Robert's friend had given him at the seminary.

"Hey!"

"Over here," her mother whispered near the road. Mahlah hooked Robert's arm and pulled him along.

"What are you two do—"He stopped and raked a hand over his face. "Don't tell me. You saw a panther…"

Her mother had drawn the pistol and watched the spot where the figure had disappeared.

Mahlah whispered, "I think it's a man but…could you tell for certain Mother?"

Her mother handed the gun to Robert and said, "As it came closer, it looked tall enough but my eyes…"

Trying to see down the slight incline, Robert stood on his toes and scanned the area, "Where did you last see him?"

Her mother pointed and whispered, "There, near that thick pine."

Robert craned his neck then lowered onto his heels again. He shrugged. "Don't see anything. Are you sure you two didn't see a cow or a deer or something?"

She exchanged glances with her mother. She was certain they had seen something else. Both shook their heads.

"Perhaps our neighbor started his Christmas celebrations early and had too much to drink…? Or maybe it's that Santa Claus fellow…"

Mahlah rolled her eyes. Robert looked over the pistol then looked back up at their mother.

"Are you certain you loaded this thing correctly?"

Indignant, her mother said, "Robert, your Grandfather, God rest his soul, took great pride in teaching me such things. I wouldn't carry the thing, or give it to you for that matter, if I wasn't certain."

They both knew better than to doubt their mother, so Mahlah nodded her reassurance to him. "Some sort of Christmas break this is turning out to be," Robert mumbled.

Mahlah clasped his arm. "Robert, just promise you won't shoot the neighbor, or anyone else for that matter…"

He gulped then nodded. The wind gusted and shook the saturated trees again. Robert wiped the large drops from his face onto his sleeve and walked across the road, hopping over puddles. After reaching the other side, he stopped and narrowed his eyes.

"Something's crawling."

As he walked toward it, Mahlah squeezed her mother's hands. Three times her mother glanced between Mahlah and Robert, and then she pulled away.

"Stay here."

Mahlah could not believe what she was hearing. "What?" she asked.

"If anything happens, lock yourself in the cabin and wait for your Father."

"But…"

She drifted toward her but her mother turned and held out her hand, "Mahlah, stay there!"

She felt like an anchor dropped off the side of a wayward boat. If she obeyed, they would not crash on the rocks, so she stayed and watched her mother follow behind Robert. Silent, they crept along the road.

A few yards from the thick pine, something cracked and screeched in the woods near Robert. Her mother and Robert covered their heads as black birds hopped free from the woods cawing and screaming. Mahlah's breath caught in her chest and her heart drummed at her temples.

Swinging his arms, Robert shouted, "Get out of here! Go, get!"

The carrion crows spread their glossy wings and hopped down the road and back into the woods. Robert raised his hand and his voice echoed back.

"Mother, wait there."

As he approached the pine tree, Mahlah realized she had drifted across the road and could now see the mound. Robert kneeled, lifted something from it, then stood and hollered back.

"Mahlah, get a blanket."

Away she ran, into the cabin. Digging through the blanket chest, her heart pounded. She wrapped a blanket around her arm and dashed out the door. Panting, she ran up the road wondering. Did she know the person? Did the panther know this person?

*****

The leaden Christmas sky made the mound difficult for Mahlah to identify from a distance. Kneeling next to it, her mother looked up.

"Don't come any closer Mahlah." Robert said walking towards her. "Hand me the blanket."

Mahlah did, then waited, and watched. The figure lay wrapped in what looked like a dirty quilt. Robert straddled the figure.

"Do you want to carry him on this one," Robert said, holding up the blanket, "or that one?"

"He already has this one under him. I just can't tell if it will hold his weight."

A him. Was it their neighbor? The dirty quilt covered the figure completely.

"Mahlah," her mother said over the pattering rain, "avert your eyes."

Without arguing, Mahlah turned away even though she wanted to see the reason. Was he still alive? Did the panther rip him to pieces? While nursing the sick during the yellow fever outbreak, she had seen some horrible sites but her mother never hid them from her. The man groaned answering one of her questions. He lived.

Her mother said, "Hurry over here Mahlah. You need to hold on at his head. If you feel the quilt rip or he starts thrashing around, we'll lower him back to the ground. Alright?"

"Yes, Mother."

The crown of the man's slender head peeped out from under the blanket she had brought. He was not old, but he was not young either. His leathery skin had an unhealthy gray hue.

"Who is he? What do you think happened to him?" she said.

Robert shrugged as he took hold of the quilt. "You don't recognize him either?"

She shook her head.

Her mother grasped the other side of the quilt and said, "He's been shot in the shoulder and I have a feeling we know who's responsible."

Mahlah gasped, picturing her Papa lying in the road like this man. She remembered what Mr. Ham Bone had told her Papa, saying he had shot the panther in the shoulder but the panther had gotten away before he could end him.

Mahlah balled the quilt in her hands. They were spaced far enough apart to produce a cradle for the man's head.

"Are you ready?" asked Robert and she nodded. "On the count of three then… One, two, three…"

As they lifted the man from the mud, he groaned and rolled his head back and forth, "Let me die. I'm no good, no good…"

"Hush now, hush…" Mahlah said as they shuffled toward the cabin.

Mahlah glanced past the crossroads, hoping to see her Papa returning, but deep down she knew he was not there. Robert caught her attention.

"Wait, wait…," he said. All three stopped. "Put him down."

They gently lowered the man. Robert gathered the trailing blanket and tucked it up and around the man again, with extra care around his hips and thighs. How odd, thought Mahlah.

"Robert, I'm a grown woman. I can handle seeing a gunshot wound."

"We know." her mother said, taking hold of the quilt again, "It isn't the wound your brother is worried about. The man is stark naked."

Mahlah dropped the quilt and the man's head thudded on the ground.

"Mahlah!" her mother said scowling at her. "Careful. People can do strange things when they lose a lot of blood…"

Robert cleared his throat, "So can crazy people," he said.

Her mother shook her head and said, "To the cabin, now, or the only thing this man will be is a transitioning soul!"

As gray as the man was, she believed her mother was correct. The urgency took hold of Mahlah then. She realized how fast they needed to move. After counting to three again, they made their way to the cabin. The man groaned as they squeezed through the threshold. They laid him on the floor next to the fireplace.

Her mother lowered the blanket enough to see the gaping wound. Only a little blood seeped from the jagged rip. To her surprise, his chest rose slow and steady, not shallow or rapid like she had expected from a bloodless man.

"Robert," her mother said, "find some pants for this man. And Mahlah, I need towels, a water basin and brandy."

Robert emerged from his room as Mahlah placed the brandy and a basin next to her mother, on the floor.

Her mother looked up at her. "Now, get your father's bedroll and another blanket, but stay in the bedroom till we call you."

"Why?"

Robert held out some long underwear and raised an eyebrow.

"Oh," Mahlah said as her cheeks warmed. "I forgot."

Inside her mother and father's bedroom, she reached under the bed and took hold of her Papa's old bedroll. A loud sharp groan startled her and she hit her head on the bedframe.

"Is everything alright?" she hollered.

"Yes," her mother hollered back, "I think he's coming around."

Not knowing if having the unknown man conscious was a good thing or not, she lit the lamp on the bedside table and pushed back the encroaching dark. After pulling another blanket out of the trunk, someone knocked on the bedroom door.

Robert hollered, "You can come out now."

On the floor by the fireplace, her mother wiped the mud from the man's neck and shoulder. Shuddering, he asked, "Wh-where am I?" Then he winced.

"I am Mrs. Henry Pritchard, the Parson is my husband. You are in our cabin."

The man swallowed as if it hurt to do so.

"Would you like some water or brandy?"

"B-brandy p-please."

Her mother propped up his head and held the cup to his lips. After two gulps, he pushed it away. Next to him, Mahlah unrolled the bedroll then threw a log on the fire. The warmth had faded the gray in his cheek already. Maybe the man was only cold. Robert stood to the side with his arms folded across his chest, eyeing the man, when someone hollered from outside.

"Halloo!"

Mahlah looked at her mother.

"It's Papa!"

Her mother's shoulders relaxed and she whispered, "Thank you, Jesus."

Robert shrugged on his coat and strode out into the rain to meet him. The man lifted his head and peered around the room, still shaking. To Mahlah's surprise, he gave the air two quick sniffs.

"Did you say I made it to the Parson's cabin?" he asked.

Her mother propped up his head again and he drank as she answered. "Yes, do you know my husband?"

The man shook his head.

"Do you know the cabin?"

A tear rolled down his cheek but he did not answer. He turned and watched the fire. Mahlah glanced at her mother. She looked worried. A moment later, her Papa strode through the doorway. Excited and relieved, she ran over and hugged him tight.

"Now, who do we have here?"

Inside the door, her Papa sat on the bench and Mahlah helped pull off his boots. Not one time did the man glance at them.

He did not answer either. She shrugged when her Papa looked at her. With his eyebrow raised, he wiggled his toes and shrugged back. Standing, her Papa stretched then walked over to her mother and the man. After hanging his coat by the fire, her Papa glanced at the man, then looked at her and her mother and shook his head. Apparently, he did not know the man either.

He stooped down next to her mother, lifted the dressing from the wound and said, "You have lost a lot of blood, friend. Is there someone I can send for? Do you have family here abouts?"

Clenching his jaw, the man shook his head.

"Do you have a name?"

His jaw stayed clenched and he closed his eyes. A tear rolled down his cheek and he said, "None that matters anymore."

Her Papa put a hand on the man's good shoulder. "That is hard to believe, friend. Now I know you do not feel like talking but how did you end up this way? Did someone do this to you?"

The man looked into her Papa's eyes then moved his good forearm over his face. Was he crying? The blanket slid down and Mahlah could see something written on his chest. Her Papa noticed it also. She stood on tiptoes and craned her neck to get a better look. In big black letters, someone had scrawled *Lucy* over the man's heart. Mahlah watched her Papa for signs of recognition. This man had to be the lost sailor, Ham Bone and Lucy's Earl.

Her Papa helped her mother up and led her just inside their bedroom. Mahlah's heart pounded. What were they going to do? Did Mr. Ham Bone shoot him? When her Papa waved her over, she almost danced for joy.

They hugged and her mother asked, "How did you get back so early?"

"Ran into the Sherriff along the way. I explained things and he decided to escort Mr. Ham Bone home. Funny thing is, the Sherriff's seen the panther following Mr. Ham Bone also."

On the floor, the man turned toward them, obviously listening.

Her Papa pulled them further into the room and whispered, "Did he have any belongings with him?"

Mother shook her head and said, "Only the quilt. We had to put Robert's long johns on him, for heaven's sakes!" She squeezed Papa's hands and whispered, "You don't think Mr. Ham Bone shot him, do you? You saw how he drew on the children…"

Enthusiastically, Mahlah nodded and said, "Papa, he has to be Earl. Did you see the tattoo? It says Lucy…"

Mother looked at her with Papa narrowing his eyes at her. Mahlah gulped and her mother asked, "Who are Earl and Lucy?"

She stared at them both, trying to think of an answer when the front door banged open. Robert stepped inside, wet as ever.

"My, it's gotten cold out there."

He walked to the fireplace and hung his coat next to her Papa's.

"Well you look better…," he said to the man. "It's a Christmas miracle that we found you when we did."

The man huffed then began to cough. Her Papa waved a finger at her.

"We will discuss this later, young lady." and he strode away.

Kneeling next to him again, her Papa lifted the man's head while Robert held the cup to his lips. The coughing eased. After tucking the muddy quilt under him, her Papa pulled the bedroll closer.

"Ladies, let us roll him onto the bedroll and off this quilt."

Wide eyed, the man shook his head. "No," he said, "you can't! It's the only thing I have left…"

*****

It took close to a half an hour to assure the man that the quilt could stay next to him if he moved to the bedroll. After they cleaned his wound and changed his bandage, her Papa said a prayer of thanks for their last Advent meal. He thanked the Lord for sparing their new friend. Mahlah hoped the man would at least acknowledge the prayer, but he only stared into the fire. The man did not ignore the lentil and mushroom soup, though. He did not even use a spoon; he just slurped it from the bowl, and then fell asleep.

"Will you go for Doctor MacDowell?" Mahlah asked her Papa and Robert in the kitchen.

"Can't." her Papa said. "The fog and mist are too bad. I'm lucky I made it home."

Mahlah bit her lip. As they stared at the man, she whispered, "Do you think he will die?"

Robert showed interested in that question. Her Papa paused and lit his pipe. The smoke swirled in front of him and Mahlah imagined that the thoughts inside his head swirled the same way.

"He is not bleeding all that bad now, but I don't know… He does not seem to care if he lives or dies. And sometimes, that's all that matters."

Her Papa puffed on the pipe faster and faster, and then stopped.

"Well, it is getting late and your Mother needs sleep after all the commotion and Christmas baking today. I will stay with our friend. Robert, if I tire, I will wake you."

Her mother kissed him on the cheek then hugged them goodnight. Glancing at the man, her mother touched her Papa's cheek and whispered.

"Do not fall asleep." Glancing at the man again, she hesitated then said, "There is something missing in that man's eyes and I …" she shook her head.

Her Papa smiled, "Don't worry my dear. You and the children are my most precious things. I will guard you with life and soul."

Her mother smiled, "Let's hope it never comes to that." She kissed him on the cheek again and went into their bedroom.

Robert crept over to the man then bent and stretched out the filthy quilt. Careful not to wake the man, he looked over the bloodstains and mud. Mahlah and her Papa walked closer and her Papa gestured to Robert to put it down and come away.

"What are you doing?" her Papa asked him.

"I am trying to figure out what is so important about that quilt. I do not think he has any gold or silver sewn into it. It has no weight."

Mahlah stared at the intertwining rings of patchwork and whispered, "It is a wedding quilt. It must have been his and Lucy's."

With gaping mouths, Robert and her Papa glanced at the quilt and then her.

"I thought you didn't know who he is…," said Robert, "and who is Lucy?"

From under his eyelashes, her Papa glared at her as the man groaned then squirmed under the blankets.

"See," Mahlah whispered, "he recognizes the name."

"Do you two know the man or not?"

Her Papa sighed then said, "We may have heard of the man but we have no proof."

Mahlah could not believe what she heard. "Proof? You mean that having Lucy's name tattooed across his chest is merely a coincidence?"

"Enough Mahlah—"

"But Papa, Mr. Ham Bone said—"

"I believe it is time for bed, young lady."

"But—"

Her Papa grabbed her arm and pulled her to her bedroom door. "Young lady," he whispered through his teeth, "what Mr. Ham Bone said to me, he said in confidence. When this man is ready to tell his story, he will do so. It is not your place to do it for him."

Ashamed, Mahlah stared at her shoes.

"I am sorry, Papa. I do not know why I listened. I know better, honest. Please do not let this ruin your Christmas. Robert might not be able to come home next year and I feel like our lives are changing too quickly. Like, something horrible is just around the corner."

Firm and endearing, her Papa hugged her and whispered, "That thing around the corner is called adulthood. And it is only horrible if you do not embrace it." He squeezed her and chuckled,

"The Lord will see you through it." He held her out and looked her in the eyes, "Soon, you will meet a man who will do whatever it takes to keep you safe. Even if you do not always understand his reasons, you will trust him. Then, that corner will not be as horrible. I promise."

He squeezed her again and warm tears ran down her cheeks.

"I love you Papa."

"I love you too."

She turned to walk into her room but the odd feeling in her stomach made her stop. Even though the man loved Lucy enough to tattoo her name over his heart, Mahlah saw the same thing lacking in the man's eyes that her mother did.

"Papa?"

"Yes, child?"

"Mother is right. Don't fall asleep."

Her Papa straightened his back and his face. "I won't," he said.

"And neither will I," said Robert from behind him, "even if I have to eat some of Mother's apple cake to do so."

In bed, after mulling over her Papa's words, Mahlah tossed to one side trying to make sense of the man's nakedness. Then, when she could not imagine a rational explanation, she tossed to the other side and imagined baby Jesus shaking his head and waving his finger to shame her for spying. Finally, after wondering why she did not feel what her Papa described for a good man like Vikar, she gave up on sleep.

After donning her robe, Mahlah listened at the bedroom door. She prayed she would not hear her Papa snoring.

Instead, her Papa's voice said, "…going out into this cold and misty rain is sure death in your condition."

Something scraped across the floor violently. Mahlah's heart pounded, she knew she should not listen but she needed to be certain the man could be trusted and that her Papa was all right.

"Oh Parson," the man said, sounding disappointed, "until I rip Ham Bone into pieces, like I asked in the bargain we struck, the fiend won't let me die."

Mahlah heard footsteps then shuffling. She huddled behind the door, holding her breath. A moment later, the rocking chair rungs clicking against the floor and her Papa said, "So what you are saying is that you wish to turn from this destructive path but you do not know how?"

The man grunted in frustration. "Parson," he said, "nothing in that book will change what I done." The man paused, "I am too deep now, too --"

"Friend, if we still live, it is never possible to be too deep or too far away from the Lord. He will always welcome us back."

The man laughed an eerie, hopeless laugh then said, "Even without a soul?"

"Yes," her papa said, "even if you believe you have sold your soul."

Every hair on Mahlah's body tingled. It was one thing to hear these stories second hand, but to have someone under your roof that truly believed they had no soul was indescribable.

"Parson," the man paused, and then said, "when the weather clears, pack up your family and move far away from here.

Better yet, avoid anyone you come across who knows of this place."

She heard shuffling towards the door and then her Papa spoke again. "Before you leave, let me read you a short passage from the good book."

The shuffling stopped.

"If I listen, you won't follow or try to stop me?"

Her Papa sighed, then said, "It is your path, friend. I will not attempt to stop you."

The man laughed another wicked laugh. "Don't think ye'd have much luck in stopping me, but, it's Christmas… I will let you say your peace, for my mother's sake… She always liked Christmas."

The pages rustled and she imagined her Papa holding the large black Bible on his lap. She tried to imagine what her Papa might read, but before she could, the rustling quieted and he began.

James 4 6:10

But he giveth more grace. Wherefore he saith, God resisteth the proud, but giveth grace unto the humble. Submit yourselves therefore to God. Resist the devil, and he will flee from you. Draw nigh to God, and he will draw nigh to you. Cleanse your hands, ye sinners; and purify your hearts, ye double minded. Be afflicted, and mourn, and weep: let your laughter be turned to mourning, and your joy to heaviness. Humble yourselves in the sight of the Lord, and he shall lift you up.

The book slapped shut but no one spoke. Mahlah waited, wondering what the man, who believed he had sold his soul, might make of the reading. Then, he spoke.

"You dog eared that one when you found out you was moving here, didn't you Parson?"

"Yes," her Papa said, "as a matter of fact, I did."

Holding her breath, Mahlah realized that this was the moment her Papa had prepared for; the reason he had moved to the crossroads.

"So what is it you're saying, Preacher? That if I be a good boy and keep my hands clean, God 'll make the Devil give back my soul?"

Her papa sounded desperate. "The Devil cannot take a man's soul unless the man dies unrepentant," he said.

After a long pause, the man laughed. He laughed so hard, that he coughed as if his lungs were shredding.

"Here," her papa said over the coughing, "drink this."

Mahlah pressed her face against the door, hoping to hear better. A moment later, the door rattled and something hit the floor outside. She jumped back, frozen in her tracks. On the floor, under the door, a small pool of liquid crept into her room.

Louder, the man said, "After Ham Bone took my Lucy, he beat me till I didn't recognize myself in the looking glass. For three days, they let me lie in the mop closet of the ordinary, hoping and praying she'd leave him and come find me. On the third day, when I could walk again, Lucy found me. She opened the door, clutching this quilt. Our wedding quilt. I thought she was gonna leave him and come with me, but she only handed me the quilt and said she couldn't. Ham Bone would find us, she said, an we'd never be safe cause he's stronger and a better shot."

A foot scrapped the floor outside her door and something blocked the light. She held her breath.

She knew it was her papa when he said, "Did you talk to the magistrate? See if you have any legal rights in the matter?"

The front door rattled opened and Mahlah pressed her ear closer. Muffled, as if speaking through his teeth, the man said, "Preacher, why would I do that when I could come here and ask for the power to rip Ham Bone to pieces, to rip him apart and crush his bones in my..."

The man's talk turned to weeping then faded. Her papa's steps moved quickly to the front door. Shivering, she prayed he would just let the man go and latch the lock. With no sound coming through the door, she ran to the window and peeped between the shudders. Her worst fear stood outside her window. Her papa had followed the man.

"Preacher," the man's voice echoed, facing the crossroads. "You gotta be careful how you say things, you know. I never really wanted this... I watch the two of 'em and try to stay away, but the need comes over me and... I ain't got no-body and no-place to go. It's like someone fixed my rudder an' I can't unfix it till I crash on the rocks."

Hugging himself, her papa said, "Remove yourself from the temptation then. Go to the other end of the bay, go to sea, or take a train. If you need clothes and money..."

It was too dark to see the man's expression as he turned and looked at her papa, but she could see Robert's long johns hanging off his hips and his eyes shining above them.

"Do you think that will help the emptiness I feel? I figure it's gotta be 'cause my soul's missing and God don't want nothing to do with me anymore."

She gasped as her papa took two steps closer to the man and said, "God does not turn from us, my friend. We turn from God. Work hard at keeping His ways, and ask His forgiveness. You will feel His grace again."

The man took a deep breath and cradled his wounded arm. "I hope you've got the right of this Preacher, cause if not…" He turned and sprinted into the mist.

"Wait!" yelled her papa while running after him.

Mahlah ripped open her bedroom door, and ran out of the front cabin.

"Papa, Papa," she yelled from the steps.

"Over here!"

While draping something over his wrist, her papa walked out of the mist. Robert and Mother ran to the door.

"What?" yelled her mother, "What's happened?"

Soaking wet, her papa shook his head as he pushed them back into the cabin.

"He's gone, into the mist. I couldn't see anything but this…"

Her papa held up Robert's muddy long johns then, her mother picked up the quilt in front of the door.

"You mean he's completely…?"

"Yep," said her papa, "If he does not freeze to death, it will be a Christmas miracle."

The next morning, only a few families attended Christmas service outside, in the mud. Her papa asked the Sherriff and the other men to search the woods for Earl but no one looked for long. The rain had washed away his tracks and the cold damp air, along with Earl's condition, did not leave them much hope.

"Sorry, Parson," the Sherriff said. "I'll stop in on Ham Bone and Lucy on the way home, and see if they know anything."

After thanking the parishioners and wishing them all a merry Christmas, Mahlah and her mother watched her papa and Robert head back into the woods for one more look. When they were out of site, Mahlah and her mother walked into the cabin.

They placed the Christmas roast over the fire then peeled and chopped potatoes, carrots, beets and celery. As their preparations slowed, Mahlah and her mother sat in front of the fire and listened to the meat hiss as it cooked. Her mother picked up Lucy and Earl's wedding quilt and held it up for a better look.

"Well," her mother said, "I guess we should soak this and clean it. Just in case Earl comes back for it. I cannot believe that he forgot it after all the fuss he made over it."

Mahlah could not believe Earl chose to run around naked, but she did not think he could still be alive either. It did feel good to do something kind for someone, though. As they looked over the fabric reciting the best remedies for blood, mud, and grass stains, her mother got up and carried it to the window for a better look.

In the center and along the tattered edges, her mother pointed.

"Mahlah? What does this and this resemble to you?"

Mahlah ran her hand over the marks and gasped.

"Those look like large teeth snags. Sort of like Mrs. Jennings's cat used to do to the arm of her sofa." Then, Mahlah held the quilt closer to the window. "And these. They look like very large paw prints."

When she looked up, her mother stood with a defiant look on her face, staring out the window at the crossroads.

"Mother, do you think—"

Her mother pulled the quilt out of her hands and said, "Think? Do you want to know what I think?"

Mahlah hesitated, "Yes Mother, I do."

High strung, her mother walked over to the kitchen and lifted the washbasin off its hook on the wall.

"I think we should boil lemons then leave this to soak overnight."

Clanging around the kitchen, her mother sang loud, as Mahlah watched in disbelief.

The first Noel the angel did say
Was to certain poor shepherds in fields as they lay
In fields as they lay, keeping their sheep,
On a cold winter's night that was so deep.

The marks had to be a coincidence. Maybe they had scared the panther away when they found him. She wanted to show her papa and hear his opinion but her mother would not stop singing or scrubbing. Before Mahlah knew it, the Christmas roast had cooked to perfection and her mother had the quilt soaking in the basin, dissolving the last traces of Earl.

Tea with a Hussy

By

Jeanne Johansen

I was born into a family who believed in rules. My grandmother Mary Helen called it "comportment" and it included a strict set of instructions which must be followed. Failure resulted in punishment and the ever looming possibility one's social rank would suddenly be plunged into an empty elevator shaft where you tumbled ass over elbow down to some dank place, never to be heard from again. That – and the shame one would bring to one's family for generations to come – was enough to keep me in line. Usually.

Well, sort of. My name is Mary Elizabeth Duncan. I was born in Richmond, Virginia right after World War I. My mother, born in 1921, married my father, Lt. Col. Harrison Bertram Duncan, in December 1941. It would be two days later that the Japanese attacked Pearl Harbor, leaving the newlyweds to start their marriage without a honeymoon. They managed somehow to get together long enough to conceive my older brother Thompson before dad was off to war, and the family didn't see him again until it ended in 1945.

When the war ended, Momma and Father made up for lost time. My brother Timothy was born in 1947, and in 1948 I came along. Father had been promoted to Colonel and had received some sort of award he was quite secretive about. My older brother called it the Ghost Award because no one in the family talked of it, except to say he had it and President Truman had awarded it. Father was someone you never questioned. He would invite us into his study, one at a time, to discuss our "comportment". He kept a book on his desk where he had written everything he wished to discuss. When he was finished, he closed the book and the conversation was over.

When I was six years old, I decided to be brave and ask him about the ghost award. He slammed the book shut and told me our conference was finished. I never asked him again.

Grandmother pulled some strings to get Father stationed in Richmond. We were all living at the family residence in Ginter Park – one of those old red brick mansions with lots of rooms and scary places. The first floor entrance had a crystal chandelier the lighted the entrance. The formal dining room was to the right. There was a button on the floor where Grandmother sat that, when pressed, summoned the servants. To the right of the entrance was the parlor, with another grand chandelier in the center of the room, a massive fireplace with carved woodwork and a mantle that held our Christmas stockings every year. The ceilings were over 10 feet, and dentil crown molding joined the walls and ceiling.

There were four bedrooms and three bathrooms on the second floor. Mother and Father's bedroom had a fireplace and a connecting bathroom. My grandmother and I shared a room. My two brothers shared a room, and the spare room was left for overnight guests. The third floor was the servants' quarters, with a stairway running down the back of the house to the kitchen. We had servants of the "colored variety" as my grandmother called them. They were seen but not heard and that was how she wanted it.

In the summertime we packed up and drove approximately one and one half hours due East to the small community of Deltaville. We had a summer house there, a big two-story rambling monstrosity that took up a large sand beach on the Chesapeake Bay. I loved the old house – it has survived the Hurricane of 1930 and other such natural and unnatural disasters. We all went – servants, brothers, grandmother, and momma – everyone except Father. He would come sporadically – and I remember his white legs and bare chest moving gently with the tides as he floated in the waters of the bay. I always worried about him out there because our family compound was located at Stingray Point where Captain John Smith nearly lost his life. I was vigilant standing on that beach, never noticing the hot sun but certain to look out for stingrays that might be after Father.

My time in Deltaville was magical, but it was always summer, and always warm. It never occurred to me that one day in the near future I would be there for Christmas, or that my life would be so completely changed I wouldn't want to be anywhere else.

Included in our family compound were my two maiden aunts – great aunts to be precise. They were Grandmothers sisters who never married, but chose to live in Deltaville rather than the family home in Richmond. They managed the compound for the family, and received free board and a stipend in exchange for managing the property. "Better to pay family than some fool stranger who will just muck it up," my Grandmother tell our accountant when he complained about writing checks.

Our arrival was always the same. We would arrive around noon, starving and anxious to get out of the cramped car. My aunts would make certain they were out in the Chesapeake Bay deadrise, a traditional fishing boat used in the Chesapeake Bay. Watermen would use a deadrise year round for everything from crabbing and oystering to catching fish or eels. My Aunt Maddie and Aunt Bella were no exception. They wore trousers at all times, and didn't give a damn what anyone thought

Bella would always see us first, wave and then head in to shore. They were always covered in something smelly, and would grab my grandmother first, covering her with the fish guts or whatever happened to be on their clothing. Once, Grandmother attempted to outrun them, charging up to the house. She was no match for her sisters, who tackled her half way. They were in much better shape as they worked like the men on the bay, fishing and harvested clams with huge tongs from the deck of their dead rise boat. My aunts laughed hysterically, while Grandmother got up, dusted off her pencil thin skirt and said, "Thank God you decided to stay out here and not live in Richmond. What would the neighbors think?"

My Aunts were so entertaining I didn't think to miss my friends at home or the new invention of television. The blue sky sparkled above me during those summer days, as I learned all sorts of new skills. One day I lay flat on my belly on the dock out back, exactly as Aunt Maddie instructed.

"You've got to have the chicken neck tied on like this," she explained, tightening the knot that held the meat. Below me the water swirled, a lazy sound that guaranteed treasures were waiting in the bay for my discovery. "And hold it like this."

With one hand on the string, I hung over the edge of the dock and dangled the chicken in the water. "Is this good?" I didn't want to sound anxious, but I did want to do it right. This wasn't something I could practice in Richmond.

"Perfect," Aunt Bella hollered from the end of the dock. The two women were fussing over their own fishing line, bending down and taking care to use the right bait. I could see how their outfits were more practical than any of the other women might wear; after all, who in their right mind could fish wearing a dress?

There was a tug on the string and I pulled the line up. The chicken neck was gone, but I'd gotten a nice, big crab, my first of the day.

"Let me see," Aunt Maddie called. I held it up for her to have a look, and she nodded at me. Tossing the crab into my bucket, I hurried to tie another piece of chicken onto the string. I was determined to fill that bucket.

After a while, I heard the footsteps of Aunt Bella coming toward me on the dock. Her body shadowed me as she looked into my bucket. After a moment of silence, she spoke. "You know, there's a few in there we have to throw back."

"Why?" I'd worked hard for those crabs, I wanted to keep my bucket full.

"They're too small. You have to give them a chance to get big. It's important to know when to throw them back."

It was during those long summer days my aunts taught me an important lesson: not everything you catch is a keeper.

In the late afternoons, I went with them on the deadrise to put up the crab pots we had set out in the morning. The crab pots were a square cage made from galvanized poultry wire and a bait box. My Aunts had met Benjamin Franklin Lewis of Harryhogan, Va. who invented the crab pot in the middle 1930's and he had helped them make their first ones. It replaced the trot line they used to use. They now had 41 pots we put out every morning, their colorful buoy floats marking their location. At dusk we would harvest them, bringing the catch back just in time for dinner.

One of the many things my two maiden aunts argued about was how to prepare the crabs. Maddie preferred the "cook 'em then clean 'em" method, layering them in a huge pot, covering them with beer and Old Bay seasoning and steaming them outside. Bella preferred the "clean 'em then cook 'em". She would stand at the outside sink, remove the apron with her fingers, remove the outer shell, wash off the guts, crack them in half and then put them in boiling water. I ate them both ways. My grandmother preferred Bella's method as it kept the table cleaner. She also made Maddie hide the beer – just in case one of the Baptists might happen by and see we had liquor at the house. Grandmother seemed especially concerned that Corrine Davis might stop by. She was the official Deltaville scandalmonger. I didn't realize it at the time, but what Corrine thought and said mattered to most of the residents of Deltaville, and it would matter to me too at Christmas. She was a bigwig in the local Baptist Church and belonged to the Women's Christian Temperance Union. If she discovered beer in our house, it would be all over town by morning.

Maddie thought this was quite funny. "When we take one Baptist out on the deadrise, he'll have a couple of beers with us. If we have two Baptists on the boat, our former drinking buddy suddenly becomes a teetotaler." To appease my Grandmother and protect her "reputation", she hid the beer in a safe place.

All summer we lived off the bountiful Chesapeake Bay. We traded the crabs my aunts didn't sell with our neighbor for corn and potatoes. We swapped stories and fish with the local farmers for their bounty. No one went to the grocery story – there was always a farmer with eggs or milk or chickens or homemade sausage – no end to food that came right to our door. The Chesapeake Bay was pristine back then, with crab and fish and oysters – all there for the taking. It never occurred to me to wonder if food was as plentiful once the weather turned. If they couldn't fish, where did they get the food to survive when the cold winter came?

I asked my Aunt Maddie once when we were clearing the outside table after dinner why she had never married. "Never met the right man," she said, looking at me without blinking. It usually meant she was lying, but I didn't say anything. She didn't speak for a while, just scrubbed the dishes in the old cast iron sink, dipped them in the pot of hot water and handed them to me to dry. She scrubbed harder than usual, as if to distract me from my thoughts. Finally she dropped the dishrag into the soapy water and turned to me. "Mary Liz, never settle. I am not someone who wants to cater to a man, have his children and find myself tending to a bunch of servants so I don't have to make my own way. Now, I love your grandmother. She is my sister, but she went her way and Bella and I went ours. She was always believing you had to beg permission so folks would think highly of you." She stopped and looked at me. "Now, I'm not telling you to disobey, but I always felt it was better to beg forgiveness than ask permission. Oh, and to learn to fetch and carry your own firewood honey. Learn to do it and you won't be sorry." Then she picked up the dish rag and went back to her pots.

*****

In 1957 everything changed. It was the day after Thanksgiving, and Maddie and Bella had even consented to come to Richmond for two days to celebrate with us. My Uncle Teddy had joined us. We had a huge dinner – turkey with cornbread stuffing, ham, mashed yams, rolls and more things I cannot even remember. We were stuffed after the meal, but rather than let us stay inside and sleep we were told to go out and play.

Uncle Teddy was my mother's youngest brother. He had been in the Navy in World War II and was stationed in the Pacific. Teddy was 32, but acted like a kid.. He was my mother's favorite brother, and loved to rough house with us.

I remember it was in the 50's on November 29th and we were allowed to run outside with just our sweaters on. It was 2:40 in the afternoon and I had just thrown a huge dirt clod at my brothers who were teasing me about having to wear a dress. "Don't get those ruffles on your panties dirty," they were yelling at me. The house in Ginter Park had rolling grass lawns, and my eldest brother decided I needed a good roll down one. He clipped me from behind, sending me rolling down the slope toward the street below.

Uncle Teddy walked out on the front porch just as I was headed for the thoroughfare and oncoming cars who would have never expected a girl in her Sunday best to fall from the sky onto the hood of their car.

Sensing they had put me in peril, my two idiot brothers ran after me, trying to catch me and pull me back from the street.. Teddy, however, jumped from the porch and somehow propelled himself down the hill trying to catch up with me, a nearly impossible feat as I was now flying midair into oncoming traffic.

"Stop," the three of them yelled. "Stop! Please." The sound of cars hitting their brakes broke the tranquility of the afternoon quiet. My uncle caught me in the middle of the road and tossed me to safety just as an approaching car hit him full on, killing him instantly.

The funeral was the following week. Aunt Maddie and Aunt Bella stayed to help my grandmother. My father, soon to be deployed to someplace called Viet Nam, made the arrangements. His brother and wife moved into the house to help with all of the things that happened with a death in a big family.

Southern funerals are like no other. First, you have the viewing where the deceased is laid out in a casket, in his or her Sunday best, complete with full make-up and looking like any minute they could stretch their arms and sit up. There was a family story that one of our distant relatives insisted on being "laid to rest" face down in the casket – just to see if someone would life him up by his shirt collar to make certain it was him.

Baptist funerals can last two or three days, with the family sitting by the coffin and receiving mourners. At least at a Catholic wake you can drink and tell funny stories about the deceased. No drinking and no jokes when it is a Baptist viewing.

The funeral was on a Friday. I didn't want to go, begging and pleading with my grandmother who finally said to me, "There are unpleasant things in your life, girlie! This is a calamity and you will have many others in your life. Now get dressed." I call it my grandmothers "Always Go To The Funeral" speech because for many years to follow that's what she would say to me when someone passed. "Even if it was inconvenient, it means the world to the family." I took her to a lot of them before she died on News Years Day 2000.

The church was packed with funeral flowers Those lilies – a lot of them – were everywhere. We had to sit on the front row in front of everyone.

There are some things I should tell you about a Southern funeral. I call it the four "Fs":

1.   Funeral Food – No one eats better than a Southern funeral attendee. Funeral food is always out in abundance. Everyone has a funeral dish they are famous for – fried chicken, green bean casserole, pound cake, deviled eggs – all supplied in dishes with the donors name on a piece of masking tape on the bottom so it can be returned with a thank you note after the funeral. And the food has a name like "Aunt Lura's pound cake" or "Aunt Winnie's ham biscuits". And God help the person who brings a competing dish.
2.   Family Reunion - "My, how so-and-so has grown", "Is that Billy Tom's new wife?", "Dubbin has blown up – he's fat as a pig", "Doesn't she lay nice (the deceased)". There is always a scandal with someone showing up that should not be there. My uncle's funeral was no exception.
3.   Filing in and filing out – The procession and recession is very important. Everyone parades in and out in their funeral finery. Pews in the church are reserved for the family who sit together and put petty grievances aside for at least an hour.
4.   Final Call to Repentance - Every southern funeral I attended, including my uncle's, included an "altar call". No one ever goes forward, and I have never heard anyone say they were saved at a funeral.

My uncle's service lasted a long time, and I wanted the whole thing to be over. I kept praying no one would walk forward to drag it out any longer. My prayers went unanswered, because just as the final verse of *Just As I Am* was winding down, Rev. Hastings was intoning his final plea, and I thought we were home free. It wasn't going to happen. Down the aisle came a woman who looked to be in her early thirties, and Rev. Hastings kept motioning her onward. She was accompanied by a boy who looked to be about my age. She held his hand as they came forward.

My grandmother, Aunt Maddie, Aunt Bella and I heard the entire congregation in union, as if they were a well-rehearsed church choir singing Handel's *Hallelujah Chorus*, blending their voices as if they had suddenly become one human being, whisper two words:

The Hussy!

*****

My poor mother – she was so torn up she refused to talk to me or my brothers. She stayed in bed for days and refused my grandmother's attempts to feed her. My father's tour to View Nam was postponed indefinitely. I begged and pleaded with my Aunts to go to Deltaville with them. Since I was having nightmares and refused to go outside and had begun wetting the bed, my parents and grandmother finally relented. My two brothers, guilt ridden over our uncle's death, stayed in Ginter Park. "It will give her mother time to heal," Maddie said.

So, I was to spend Christmas in Deltaville.

Now, Deltaville in the summer is a lovely place. Deltaville in the winter is atrocious. The beautiful Chesapeake Bay, a vibrant blue in summer, is a grey foaming monster ebbing, flowing and freezing everything in sight. The summer folk have returned to their homes elsewhere, and what is left is the "born here's" who are firmly rooted and not going much of anywhere.

My aunts decided to make the best of things, even suggesting we tromp into the woods and find a Christmas tree and decorate it. It was freezing outside, had rained and the sky threatened snow. The ground was very slippery because the sun never reached it to dry it out. I fell once or twice, getting up and brushing off the smelly mud from my clothes. "How about this one?" Aunt Maddie asked. "What's the matter with you – that's a wretched tree," Aunt Bella answered.

They hadn't had a Christmas tree in years, had no decorations to speak of, and the woods had all of the wrong kind of pine trees. Nevertheless, we finally found a Norfolk Pine, hauled it home and set it upright in a pot of soil. We popped popcorn and strung it with needle and thread, making garlands for the tree. Aunt Bella found some cranberries and we strung those too. If the tree had been blue, it would have looked like an American flag.

Aunt Maddie found a couple of strands of primary color Christmas lights for the tree, and fortunately they were the kind that stayed lit if one burned out because about a third of them weren't working. When the tree was done, it looked pretty good.

I know now what an effort it was for my two aunts to have me come live with them. In the wintertime they closed off the top floors of the house and lived downstairs to conserve fuel. There were two rooms for them and a bathroom, so I camped out in the dining room. They shoved the dining room table and chairs against the wall and made me a very comfortable bed on a cot. It was close to the radiator so I had plenty of heat. At night I would look out of the dining room window at the stars, imagining my uncle was looking back at me and wondering why in the world I would choose to spend Christmas in Deltaville, Virginia.

My Grandmother had insisted I wait to open my Christmas presents from my brothers and other relatives back in Richmond. That was fine with me, because it was usually clothes and books. I didn't care if I ever got them.

I knew my aunts were fretting over the altar call from the funeral, and were petrified I would ask the question. I heard them whispering about it in the evening when they thought I was asleep. It was a ritual – each would sigh heavily, put their book down on their lap, pull their reading glasses from their faces and say, "What will we say if she should ask about the hussy?"

Finally, I decided to relieve the suspense. I did, however, exercise some restraint and postponed asking until the first week ended.

Dinner was finished, the dishes were done and the kitchen was clean. We were sitting in the parlor, and Aunt Maddie had made a roaring fire. She and Bella were sipping brandies and I had a hot chocolate covered in huge marshmallows. We watched the flames pirouetting in the old stone fireplace. The tree was lit and I found you really didn't notice the missing bulbs after a while.

"Nice fire," I said.

They nodded in union.

"I was wondering about something that happened at Uncle Teddy's funeral."

Silence.

"It was at the end where the minister asked people to come forward and be saved."

An audible gasp.

"And that woman came up and I think her name was Miss Hussy or something like that. I think that's what I heard people saying."

Maddie went first. "No, her name is Eliza Baines Huntsman."

"I could have sworn I heard them say Hussy."

Bella was next. "They did."

"So, if her name is Huntsman then why do they call her Hussy?"

Finally Maddie spoke. "She is a Hussy. It's not her name – it's what she is."

"What's a hussy?"

"She's not a good person. Sometimes women…" My aunt stopped here as if considering whether she should continue. "Sometimes women do things with men for money, or favors or presents that nice women wouldn't do because they were brought up properly and know that kind of behavior is not acceptable."

"Do what things?" I asked.

"Just things, dear," Aunt Maddie answered uncomfortably. Both of them were staring at the fire hoping somehow the conversation would somehow incinerate itself.

I let some time pass before I spoke again. "I don't understand. What things does she do for men? Housework? Cooking? Laundry? What?"

"Listen, Mary Liz. Didn't your mamma ever tell you? You are nine years old – didn't she tell you…" She paused here, looking to her sister Bella for guidance. There was none.

Maddie continued. "…tell you about where babies came from?"

My mother had been very direct, even allowing me to see a film called *Molly Grows Up* – a sex education film we had to watch at the hospital where Momma volunteered in Richmond because no one would allow it to be shown in the schools. My brother Thompson had also told me some things. My great source of information on the subject was my friend Kathleen who had spent the summer on her uncle's farm in West Virginia. She watched cows breed, cats breed…and watched the dog have puppies. She was eager to tell me about it when she got back.

"Yes, I know all about that. What does it have to do with Miss Hussy?"

"Miss Hussy has a child, Mary Liz, and no husband. She has no job and no means of support. We don't know who her people are – she keeps to herself most of the time. And there are men from Richmond who come to see her on a regular basis at night, stay for a few hours, then leave. Her neighbor down on the Lane says they all have a BIG smile on their faces. So, just put two and two together Mary Liz. She is selling her favors."

I wasn't sure what favors had to do with anything. Sounded like she was having sex with these men and getting paid for it. Thompson said the father of one of his friends took him to a brothel and let him have sex. I figured this Miss Hussy must have been running a brothel in Deltaville.

I decided to find out.

*****

The next day was Christmas Eve. I had talked my Aunt Bella into taking me for a drive to see the Christmas decorations and stopping down on the Lane to see her friend Miss Myra before we went to services at Chesty Puller Baptist Church. Miss Myra lived cattycorner from Miss Hussy and if you sat in one of the big chairs in front of her big picture window you had a direct view of Miss Hussy's front door.

I ate Miss Myra's offering of Christmas cookies which weren't as good as my grandmothers, but were passable. I also drank the hot chocolate with red and green marshmallows.

While Miss Myra and Aunt Bella talked, I stared out the window. "My, Mary Elizabeth, you are such a lady," Miss Myra stated at one point. "Your comportment is perfect! Seen and not heard, I always say!"

"Thank you, Miss Myra," I said and continued to stare across the street.

It got dark around 5 o'clock and services were at 7:30, so if anyone was coming I figured it would be between right now and the time we had to leave.

A tall man walked up to the front stoop at the Hussy house. He was carrying two large packages wrapped in Christmas paper. He walked to the front door, knocked and was greeted by the woman I had seen walk down the aisle at my uncle's funeral. The boy was by her side and the man stooped to give him a hug. He hugged Miss Hussy too, and she ushered him inside, closing the door.

In a few minutes another man arrived. I didn't see his car, but I figured he parked somewhere else and walked. He probably didn't want someone writing down his license plate number. This time the first man came to the door, shook hands with the new arrival and ushered him inside. He, too, had packages.

Five more men arrived at the house across the street. I went outside on the pretext of looking at the stars, and could hear music and laughter coming from the house. The curtains were closed, but I could see shadows of people moving about. It looked like a party to me.

Aunt Bella called me in to use the bathroom before we left for church. It was getting close to 9 o'clock and we had to leave in about ten minutes even though it was maybe a five minute drive, counting the time it took for everyone to get into the car and for Aunt Bella to get the Packard 120 started. It was a cold natured beast, and it was a cold night, so no one knew exactly how low it would take until the engine turned over. Aunt Maddie had bought it brand new in 1942, and I think it had less than 35,000 miles on it 15 years later.

I used the bathroom and when I came back all of the people were still there. You could see their shadows dancing across the closed curtains. "No party tonight?" Aunt Maddie said under her breath as she helped me into my coat and white gloves. I didn't argue. She hadn't seen the men arrive and I didn't want her to know I was snooping. I don't know how she missed the shadows.

The Packard started right up, so off we went – up the lane to General Puller Highway to the church parking lot. We parked in the first available space. "Looks like a crowd tonight," Miss Myra said as we walked toward the door of the church.

The inside was beautiful. Soft candle light glowed on the wall sconces. The green fir tree on the podium was decorated in red bows with white ornaments and snowflakes cut from paper. Green garland framed each of the stained glass windows.

We sat in the fourth row on the right hand side. You always knew when newcomers were in the church – they sat in the wrong pew. They weren't assigned exactly, but everyone had their place.

The choir came down the center aisle and took their place in the choir loft. We sang several Christmas hymns and then the minister Rev. Sharp took to the podium.

Rev. Sharp was new to the congregation and, as my Aunt Maddie would say, the jury was out meaning they weren't too sure about him. He had been a stage actor in New York before he became a minister. He was young, unmarried and had to come to Deltaville about 6 months ago. He had been a youth pastor in his former church somewhere up north, and was highly recommended. The senior pastor, Rev. Harris, was on vacation in West Virginia, so Rev. Sharpe was standing in.

Now, Christmas Eve was an important service for the Baptist church in Deltaville. There weren't probably more than 200 people in all of Deltaville in the winter, and about half of them went to the Puller Baptist Church, and unless you were home bound and couldn't get out you were expected to be there. As a result, the sanctuary was packed, with everyone in their Christmas finery.

After the prayers, and before the offering, Rev. Sharp took to the podium. He looked out over the congregation, opened the big bible on the lectern and began to read:

"In those days Caesar Augustus issued a decree that census should be taken of the entire Roman world . And all went to their own towns to register. So Joseph also went up from the town of Nazareth in Galilee to Judea, to Bethlehem, because he belonged to the line of David. He went there to register with Mary who was pledged to be married to him and was expecting a child. While they were there, the time came for the baby to be born, and

she gave birth to her firstborn, a son. She wrapped him in cloths and placed him in a manger, because there was no room in the inn."

"I know we usually take up a Christmas offering, but tonight I am going to ask that you put your wallets and purses away. Tonight I am going to give you something. The ushers are going to come around with the offering plates and I want you to take one of the objects out. Don't worry, there are no choices here – they are all the same thing."

He paused at this point while the men who were ushering passed the offering plates down each row. Everyone took out a tea bag covered by a wrapper.

"Okay, so you are probably wondering why I am giving each one of you a tea bag. Understandable. And for those among you who have never made tea, let me tell you how to do it. First you take the wrapper off, and then you put it in a cup and add hot water. The longer the tea bag sits in the hot water, the stronger it gets. If you taste it and you don't like it, then you have to get a different flavor of tea bag. The water has nothing to do with it.

I believe that God uses problems to change us from the inside out. You can dress us up but our essential nature doesn't change. You might have your Christmas dress on, but if you have a mean spirited nature you may look okay on the outside, but on the outside you are still mean. We are basically self-centered folks who ignore the fact that God has been at work throughout history. We feel we have to do God's work or it won't get done. The thought that our 'works' are what is important just is not true. God doesn't want you to do his work – he wants to work with you.

It's our faith that is important – faith like Mary and Joseph had. In the passage I just read, we know that Mary and Joseph are engaged. Not married but engaged. We know Mary is very pregnant. I'm sure the gossip was flying back in Nazareth, a small town somewhat like Deltaville. You just don't hide something like that."

The people in the pew in front of us started squirming. My aunts and Miss Myra looked at each other. There was a slight murmuring going on in the congregation.

"So why, you might ask," he continued "would a very pregnant woman get on a donkey and travel all the way to Bethlehem. I know about the taxes, and registering in Joseph's home town – but it wasn't Mary's. Back home in Mary's home town of Nazareth they thought Jesus was illegitimate.

So, we know they were in hot water because getting pregnant and having a baby out of wedlock was a problem. Today, we sometimes react the same way toward girls who get pregnant without benefit of marriage. We shun them sometimes, call them names like…"

Rev. Sharp paused here and looked out over the group gathered to celebrate Christ's birth. It was quiet, tense and extremely uncomfortable.

"…hussy. Not that much different today than in Jesus' day. In fact, they stoned women who had sex outside of marriage. Beaten. Killed. Then, as is true now even in Deltaville, when a woman gets pregnant before marriage it is deemed to be her fault.

So who could blame Mary, despite being extremely pregnant, going with Joseph to get out of town to have that baby? Despite all of that, they were still in hot water but their faith in God brought out the best in them.

Tonight, in lieu of your offering, I gave each of you a tea bag. What I want you to do is take that bag and have tea with someone. Reach out. Maybe it will heal a rift between you and someone you once loved. Maybe it will crack that hard shell you have built around yourself. I don't want it to be comfortable; God doesn't want it to be comfortable. God wants it to be hot water."

The whole church was quiet. Even the choir sat stunned.

"Now," Rev. Sharp concluded, "tonight I am not going to have an altar call. Instead, I ask that you turn to page 375 in your hymnal and sing *O Come, All Ye Faithful.*"

After the service was over, a second service of sorts took place in the parking lot. "Do you believe it!," Miss Myra said, shaking her head. "What kind of a Christmas sermon was that!"

Everyone standing outside the church that night agreed. Except me, of course. I had already decided who I was having tea with.

The Hussy.

*****

Now, wanting to have tea with the Hussy, and actually having tea was going to be difficult. I wasn't sure how to approach it with my aunts. Fortunately, Christmas day got in the way.

Aunt Bella fixed a wonderful breakfast with muffins, scrambled eggs and homemade sausage. Even though I hated my idiot brothers, I missed them this Christmas morning. But, that all disappeared when we started opening our presents, and there were no clothes for me. There was a new rod and reel, a Kodak Duraflex Camera and 10 rolls of film, a flash attachment and carrying case. I also got my own crab pot, a book on photography, a Careers game, Sea-Monkeys and a Wham-O Flying Saucer. But the best present of all was a RCA Victor color television, 21 inches of pure pleasure. It was a present from my Aunt Maddie to my Aunt Bella, and vies versa. It cost $550 and was a huge expense for them. "It's time we got a TV," Bella said to me. "After breakfast you can help us put up the Channel Master TV Antenna."

We finished breakfast and the dishes, then got dressed in the warmest clothes possible. Aunt Maddie was on the roof, Aunt Bella was on the ladder and I was on the ground sending tools and hardware up in a bucket with a rope. After about three hours we had the antenna up and the brown rubber covered wire was passed through the window and connected to the television.

Christmas dinner was to be served at two in the afternoon. Since we usually had Christmas dinner at around 2 in the afternoon, and it was approaching that time, so we decided to stop work and eat our dinner.

Christmas in Deltaville was so different from Richmond in many ways. Even the food was different. We had oyster stew. Miss Myra joined us and brought a Jell-O mold salad (Waldorf, she called it) with nuts and apples in it. We had turkey and dressing, mashed potatoes, pea salad, Parker House Rolls, green beans Aunt Bella had canned at the end of the summer, and pickled beets. For dessert we had mince pie, pumpkin pie and Fruit for the Gods, a family tradition. After dinner, I was excused from dishes, and immediately fell asleep on the sofa in the living room.

When I woke up, it was dark outside. My aunts and Miss Myra were sitting in the kitchen drinking tea and eating their second round of dessert. I carefully folded the afghan someone had covered me with and walked into the kitchen.

"Hey, we've been waiting for you to wake up. We were just deciding what to watch tonight." Aunt Maddie tossed me the *TV Guide* with the Season's Greetings on the cover. "Patti Page has actress Terry Moore and actor Lloyd Nolan, singer Paul Anka on *The Big Record* tonight. Or maybe you would rather watch Wagon Train."

I flipped through the schedule. "How about The Adventures of Ozzie and Harriet – it has Ricky Nelson going to Hollywood."

All three smiled. "We thought you would probably want to watch Ricky," Bella said.

We decided to watch *Wagon Train* at 7:30, then *Father Knows Best. The Adventures of Ozzie and Harriet* was on at 9:00;

then we would switch over to *Kraft Television Theatre* because it was in color. After popping some popcorn, we settled in front of the new television and watched the Christmas night away.

By Friday I had come up with a plan. All of Miss Myra's favorite game shows were on in the morning. She ate lunch around noon and then slept from 2-4 pm before watching *Queen for a Day* at 4 pm. "You know," I said to my aunts over breakfast, "I was thinking maybe I would go and spend the day with Miss Myra. She gave me the beautiful hat, scarf and mittens she hand knitted for me and since I don't have any money to buy her a present I was thinking maybe I would go over and give her a pedicure and manicure and maybe fix her lunch. What do you think?"

They were smiling beatifically at me. My aunts were really into this Christian service thing and donated every year to the Baptist Missionary Fund. At one time, when they were younger, both had thought about going on a mission but something happened to change their minds and they never made the trip.

"What a wonderful idea! Let me go call Miss Myra…or would you rather?"

"No, Aunt Bella – you can call her. I'll do the dishes then go get ready. Would you mind driving me?"

"Not at all, dear. And we'll do the breakfast dishes – you just go get your things together."

I felt a slight pang of guilt as I went into the bathroom and took a shower. I got dressed, got my manicure set together Momma had given to me in March for my birthday. When I went back into the kitchen, Bella was putting her coat on and getting the car keys down from the hook by the back door. "Oh, Mary Liz, she is just so thrilled you are coming over. She and Varnie never had any children, and he was an only child so all she has is her nieces and nephews who live far away. You just don't know what this means to her!"

That made me feel even worse, but I was determined to have tea with The Hussy. I put on my coat – the one I had worn to church on Christmas Eve – and checked my coat pocket for the tea bag. It was there, ready and waiting.

Once again, the Packard started on the first try. "Must be an omen," Aunt Bella stated. "It started right up on Christmas Eve and started right up for your good deed today."

We drove the three miles to The Lane in silence. I was feeling guilty. Aunt Bella was basking in my good deed.

We arrived at Miss Myra's at 10 am sharp. She was waiting at the back door for us. "Come in, won't you Bella? Have some coffee!"

"On, thank you Myra – but this is your day and I don't want to take up any of your time with Mary Liz. She has planned quite a day of beauty for you."

They both laughed as I got out of the car and walked up the steps to the back door. Miss Myra gave me a hug and I looked down at her bare feet. Her toe nails were long, yellow and looked like they would be hard as a rock. I remembered watching my Momma soaking her feet when the woman came to the house to do her manicure. Maybe that would soften then up.

I guess Miss Myra had the same thought, because she had a big porcelain wash basin sitting on the floor in the kitchen. "I think you'll have to soak my feet first," she laughed. "My nails are thick as those tongs your aunts use to pull oysters from the bottom of the Chesapeake."

She was right. We soaked and soaked and I still had a hard time with the nail nippers in my manicure kit. I filed them down afterwards and put a coat or two of Cutex nail polish on them. They looked really nice when I finished.

It was noon by now and we had our lunch. The clam chowder and grilled cheese tasted so good, especially on that cold December day.

I had a much easier time with Miss Myra's manicure and finished in time for her two o'clock nap. "Forgive me, dear – I always nap between 2 and 4. I hope you can keep yourself occupied – the television is available to you if you'd like."

"I brought a book," I lied. "I'll just read so as not to disturb you."

"Honey, nothing can keep me from my sleep. A train could drive though here and I wouldn't hear it."

I was glad to hear that. I watched her walk upstairs and waited a few minutes before tip toeing upstairs to make certain she was asleep. Then I wrapped up in my winter coat, took the telephone off the hook and slipped out the back door and, checking carefully to be certain no one was watching, slithered across the street like the snake in the Garden of Eden to have tea with The Hussy.

I knocked on the front door. I had practiced my spiel for days – what I would say, how I would say it. But when The Hussy opened the door, I blurted out "Hello – I am Mary Elizabeth Duncan from Richmond, Virginia and I brought a tea bag I got at the Baptist Church on Christmas Eve and I want to have tea with you."

The Hussy smiled. "Yes, Mary Elizabeth, I remember you from your uncle's funeral. Won't you please come in?"

And so I did. I had tea with The Hussy that day and it changed my life forever.

*****

I was back at Miss Myra's at 3:45 pm. I made certain I warmed my hands and face before she got up. I didn't want any telltale signs of having been outside.

At exactly 3:55 pm Miss Myra came downstairs. "Goodness, child – I didn't hear a peep outta you. Would you like some tea?"

"No," I sputtered. "I'm fine. But I'll fix it for you so you don't miss *Queen for a Day.*"

"How sweet," she said.

I went into the kitchen, put the kettle on the stove and rooted around for some tea. Miss Myra only had the loose kind, but she had steel pincer spoon is perfect for making a quick cup of tea. I made her a cup of water, placed the cup on a saucer and added some cookies I found in a tin on the counter. I carried the tray holding the entire offering in to her.

'Oh, thank you! I had some Tetley Tea Bags somewhere, but this is just lovely. How well you have been raised to know how to use the pincer."

"Thank you, Miss Myra." I sat quietly as she sipped and watched until the host of *Queen for a Day*, said his parting words: "This is Jack Bailey, wishing we could make *every* woman a queen, for every single day!"

My Aunt Bella picked me up in the Packard and we headed home for dinner, but not before Myra showed her the "beautiful" job I had done on her nails. "Come back anytime," she said before shutting the door and going back to her afternoon television programs.

"That was a very nice thing you did today, Mary Liz," Bella said.

"Thank you, but…" I stopped short of telling her about my afternoon. I didn't want to spoil her good mood.

114

We got home and I had to rehash the entire day with my Aunts. We laughed about her toe nails being compared to Oyster tongs. "I doubt if Myra ever touched an Oyster tong," Maddie said. "We've tried to get her out in the deadrise, but she won't do it. She says it's man's work."

We had a great dinner. I felt incredibly guilty for keeping my secret, and begged off watching television, opting instead to go to my alcove in the dining room and pretend to sleep.

The next morning I woke up with Maddie standing over my cot. "Mary Elizabeth, please get up and make yourself presentable. Then come into the parlor. Your aunt and I would like to speak with you."

Now, my aunts never called me Mary Elizabeth unless I was in trouble. I wasn't sure what had transpired after I went to bed last night as Saint Mary Liz and woke up this morning as the pariah Mary Elizabeth. Whatever it was, it was bad.

I went into the bathroom and took a shower. This was unusual for me as most nights I took one before bedtime. I dawdled as long as I could got dressed and went into the parlor as requested. There sat my two aunts, Miss Myra and her next door neighbor Corrine Davis.

Now, Corrine Davis had a reputation in Deltaville. I remembered Corrine from the funeral, and I was certain she wasn't here because she heard we had beer hidden in the house. Some people believed she could see through walls. Many a marriage in the little village had their "until death do us part" cut short due to the wagging tongue of Corrine Davis. She was everywhere at once, and if she couldn't be there in person she had her minions who reported in daily.

The four of them were seated. My two aunts occupied the sofa, and Corrine Davis sat in the wing chair to the right, Miss Myra the wing chair to the left. It left no place for me to sit, so I stood before them.

Miss Myra was shaking her head back and forth. She was the first to speak. "Very disappointed. I am so very disappointed in you, Mary Elizabeth. You came to my home under false pretenses. And about reading a book. You didn't even have a book."

My Aunt Maddie looked at Corrine Davis. "Is this the girl you saw go into Eliza Baines Huntsman's house?"

"If you mean The Hussy Eliza Baines Huntsman, yes it is." Mrs. Davis pointed a bony finger in my direction. "I saw her leave Myra's house a little after 3:30 pm. I was delivering dinner to the Widow Daniels who lives on The Lane when I saw her go into the whore house."

With the word "whore" my two aunts snapped upright. "Whore isn't a word we use around here, Corrine," Bella said with a hint of revulsion in her voice.

I decided not to wait for the inevitable question. "I did go over to Miss Huntsman's house. I went over to have tea with her with the tea bag Rev. Sharp gave us at the Christmas service. I decided since she was in hot water with all of you, I had best see what all the fuss was about."

"That Rev. Sharp is a real trouble maker," Corrine began. "Why, just last week he told me that what I do here in Deltaville as a community service is a sin. Can you imagine telling ME that my good works such as feeding the widows and orphans of this community is a sin?"

"I think he was talking about you being a chinwag," I said.

"A chinwag? A CHINWAG? Why, I never. You need to teach this girl some manners. But what do you expect from two old maids who go out in a Chesapeake Bay Deadrise and tong for oysters like men. Half the people in this community think the two of you have unusual sexual preferences, if you want to know the truth." Miss Corrine was getting up a full head of steam.

"Now, just a minute Corrine," Aunt Bella said, standing and shaking her fist in Corrine Davis' face. "That is about enough out of you. Everyone in the community has at one time or another been a victim of your community service. You are a gossip and you know it."

"I tell it like I see it, and if folks don't have anything to worry about with their behavior then they do not need to fear Corrine Davis! Besides, this is not about me. This girl," she pointed her bony finger at me again, wagging it this time, "is a liar who is consorting at her age with a hussy. Now, a girl as young as she is does not need to be seen or associate with a woman of ill repute such as that woman. She is just a child. There is plenty of time for her to find out about worldly things, but not now in the prime of her youth. These things need to be explained to you on your wedding night by your mother and not before and consorting with people such as that woman will lessen your chances for marrying a respectable man. You may do things this way in the big city of Richmond, but here in Deltaville we have higher standards."

Everyone was shell shocked Miss Davis would mention my mother. They stared at me, waiting for me to burst into tears. I didn't.

Instead, I sat down on the floor. "Mrs. Davis, my mother explained all of that to me. I know about boys, and sex and all those things. Miss Huntsman knows my mother, who is one of the finest ladies ever born. She knew her from the hospital and she came to Uncle Teddy's funeral. You are just a mean, spiteful old woman. I didn't know Mr. Davis, but as mean as you are, I'm surprised he ever had sex with you."

"Well, I have had enough!" Corrine stood up and marched toward the front door, turning to glare at all of us. "You just wait! I'll have Rev. Sharp and his new ideas out of here before any of you know it. And you," there was that finger again, "you little hussy in training, your grandmother would be mortified at your behavior."

With that she slammed the door. I watched as she drove off to bring joy and peace to someone else.

"Anyway, tonight I invited Miss Huntsman and one of the men that come to visit her over for tea. Miss Myra, I would like you here too. I think it would be nice. After all, how often do you get to have tea with a hussy?" I asked. "Is 7:30 good?"

Miss Myra didn't know what to say, but I knew darned well she'd be here.

"Oh," I added. "I'm inviting Rev. Sharp too."

*****

At precisely 7:30 pm everyone was standing on our front porch. I couldn't image what Miss Myra was thinking. All this time she lived directly across the street from the subject of our discussion this evening and here she was standing directly next to Miss Huntsman and one of her "clients". And then there was Miss Huntsman's son, who was sent off to watch television. Oh, and Rev. Sharp who I think found the whole thing quite funny.

We had made quite a bit of tea, and put out some finger sandwiches and cookies left over from Christmas dinner. We all sat around the dining room table (my cot had been removed for the occasion) and made Southern small talk. I kept seeing a car driving up and down the street, and since we were on a dead end, it was hard to miss.

I decided, as the youngest in the room, it was up to me to start the ball rolling. "I wanted you to come here tonight so you could meet Miss Huntsman and one of her friends," I began.

Miss Myra looked like she was sitting on hot coals.

"I realize I am only a 9 year old girl, but I think it is time to get some things straightened out here. So…"

Just then a car pulled on to our front lawn, a door slammed and Corrine Davis burst through the front door.

"Aha, Rev. Sharp. So this is where you are," she said as she surged through the front door. "And you," she pointed her scrawny finger at Miss Huntsman, "have no right to be in the company of proper people. And you," she turned to the man who had accompanied Miss Huntsman to the house, "you should be ashamed of paying a woman for sex. Why, Bobby Harrison – is that you? Your mother was one of my dearest friends before she passed. My GAWD what would she say knowing you were consorting with a…a…a hussy!"

Bobby stood up and offered Mrs. Davis a chair. "If my mother were here, she'd probably tell you to sit down and shut your mouth. Since she's 'passed' as you put it, I'll tell you to sit down and shut up."

Mrs. Davis dropped to the chair, speechless.

"I'd like to explain," Bobby began. "Mrs. Huntsman is the widow of our squad leader, Sargent Huntsman. There were eight of us in the squad, and we were in way over our heads. It was less than 20 degrees and there were a couple of feet of snow on the ground. We were greatly outnumbered. He saved my life."

"Bobby, could you fetch the tea pot in the kitchen," Aunt Maddie asked. I think she knew what Corrine Davis intended to ask, and she wanted a straight answer.

"Sure," Bobby said and he went into the kitchen to get the other pot.

"But the men coming at all hours of the night?" Miss Davis began.

"Oh, I can explain that," Miss Huntsman began. "I talked to his squad members when they visited my husband in the hospital. He was carried him back to the field hospital where they amputated his leg. He lived another 12 years, and died last year at the hospital in Richmond. Mary Liz's uncle visited where her mother volunteered. My husband was in there for about six months, and Mrs. Duncan visited him every day she was there. She was very helpful to me, even helping me with the funeral arrangements." Mrs. Huntsman stopped for a moment and wiped her eyes.

"Anyway," she continued, "His squad all came to visit him in the hospital. Two of the guys live in California, the rest of us on this end of the US. He knew he was dying and he was so worried about me. Bobby's dad owns the cottage where I am staying. I wanted to come here because my husband talked about how friendly…"

Bobby was back with the other tea pot. He paused at this point and looked at each of us.

"I don't remember any Huntsman family," Corrine said.

"He used to come with my family out here for the summer," Bobby said. "He was an orphan, living with a family right next door to our home in Richmond. We became friends, went to school together and enlisted together right after Pearl Harbor. She wanted to go someplace where she could heal."

Wow, was it quiet!

"But the altar call?" Corrine asked

"Oh, that," Mrs. Huntsman replied. "I'm Catholic and I was late for the service because we had to drive all the way from Deltaville, so I thought he was asking people to come up and say goodbye."

"But her customers. There are men coming and going all night. Where do they park, anyway?" Corrine asked.

"I told you, Mrs. Davis, they are my husband's comrades. They promised to take care of me as long as I lived. They came to the hospital every day toward the end. Now they come to the house, bring food, money – we want for nothing."

No one said anything. No one had to.

I returned to Richmond the second week of January. My brothers were nice to me – I want to say they missed me, but that would be too much of a Christmas miracle. I got the usual clothes and books, but my mother had bought me a Schwinn 24 inch girl's bike.

I went back to Deltaville that summer and every summer until I went off to college. Mrs. Huntsman became a great friend, and I stayed with her often in the little cottage on The Lane.

A lot went on over the years after "the tea with the hussy" incident, as my maiden aunts liked to call it. Word got around Deltaville that the Chinwag had gone after the widow of a World War II hero, and so no one listened to her anymore. Many a marriage was saved by that alone!

Rev. Sharp stayed on as the associate minister at Puller Baptist. He was a dynamic speaker, and brought many new people into the church. Mrs. Huntsman played the organ, and would play for services. After a while, Rev. Sharp invited her to lunch and one thing lead to another and they were married about five years after the incident.

My aunts stayed on, fishing the bay, tonging for oysters and catching crabs well into their 80s.

I went on to college, but would always come back (even for a little bit) every summer to ride in the back of the deadrise, manage the crab pots and recall my 9th Christmas where I learned that you never understand a person from a distance, that there's a lot of ugly things in this world and it's impossible to keep away from all of them and it's pretty much always better to beg forgiveness than ask permission – especially when it comes to disobeying your elders.

Oh, yeah – and I learned to fetch and carry my own firewood.

15782884R00065

Made in the USA
Charleston, SC
20 November 2012